# IMMORTAL

David Boiani

**Foundations Book Publishing**
Brandon, MS 39047
www.FoundationsBooks.net

**Immortal**
By David Boiani

ISBN: 978-1-64583-023-8

Cover by Dawné Dominique Copyright © 2020

Edited and formatted by Steve Soderquist

Copyright 2020© David Boiani

**Published in the United States of America**
**Worldwide Electronic & Digital Rights**
**Worldwide English Language Print Rights**

# Acknowledgement

I'd like to thank all my readers and followers. When I write, I open my heart and spill what's inside.

...Anything less, and the reader will know.

# Table of Contents

# Chapter One

D aniel Burton rolled off his wife and headed to the bathroom to splash cold water on his face. Their sex was always satisfying, however they'd fallen into habitual procedure since their first child, Emily, had come into their lives ten years ago. Structured time and procedure combined with stunted passion had become commonplace in their bed. Daniel studied his reflection in the mirror and his mind raced.

*Is this it? Is this all life had to offer?* he thought as he noticed the lines in his face becoming seemingly clearer by the day. As he pulled his brown sweaty bangs back, he noticed his hairline had crept further up his forehead. His stomach had protruded further while his round, hard muscles had seemingly softened and diminished. Daniel had a great life: a beautiful wife he loved, honest, intelligent children, a superb career, and a large stately home he was proud of. He even drove a prestigious, high-end, electric sports car that all his friends and colleagues coveted. He was successful in every sense of the word, so why these doubts? Why did he feel like his life was passing him by? Why did he feel he was missing out on something, some secret, about life he had yet to discover?

Daniel returned to bed, kissed Madison on the lips, turned over, and faded away with thoughts of life, death and everything in between invading his mind.


Sunlight pierced the lingering shade of the bedroom and soon Daniel's eyes opened, quickly adjusting to the bright stream of rays. He turned and glanced at Madison, as beautiful as ever, sleeping peacefully. The brightening room accented her golden hair and the soft, creamy complexion of her skin, making Daniel smile. Although many years had passed, he was still in love with her and was grateful for the strong bond they shared.

Daniel quickly jumped up and headed to the bathroom. It being a Thursday, his first lecture was scheduled for 8:30 and he was already running behind schedule. He glanced at his Rolex, which read 7:10 and the drive from his home in Hunterdon to Princeton would take forty-five minutes on an average day. He hustled into the shower, was shaved, dressed and on the road by 7:35, kissing Madison, Emily, and Logan on his way out.


"Plato said, 'Human behavior flows from three sources: desire, emotion, and knowledge.' What do you think he meant by these words, and how can we apply this thought process to our current times?"

Susan Gomes, his prized Philosophy 110-Critical Thinking Student raised her hand.

"Go ahead, Susan."

"It's the three reasons we do things. The three sources that cause our decision making to ultimately fall where it does."

"Exactly. Some are driven by an overbearing yearning to achieve, some by whatever emotional reaction they have to each incident or event, and some simply by experience and knowledge obtained through a life already lived. At times, we use each of these sources, noting in the backs of our minds how the results occur from the use of each. In today's world the most experienced, confident people use all three in combination, knowing when to use one more than the other instinctively. These people will always be the most successful, depending and varying on what each individual considers success. Susan, what would you consider success?"

"Having a healthy, caring family and making enough money to support them comfortably."

"Those are wonderful goals, however, they may not be consistent with another person's definition of success. Anyone else?"

Brian Chadwick, the class clown, raised his hand to chuckling from the rest of the class. Daniel put his hand to his forehead which brought a wave of laughter from his students.

"Yes, Brian?"

"I want to someday date a porn-star. That would complete me."

When the laughter died down, Daniel said, "On that note, we will end this lecture. Read Chapter two: *Aristotle,* for Monday's class. Everyone have an enjoyable, safe weekend and I know there are parties planned so please, if you drink, don't drive. Good day."

After his students vacated the lecture hall, Daniel sat behind his desk, taking further inventory of his life. He loved what he did. Teaching philosophy at Princeton had been a lifelong dream and surely, he considered himself a success in his own mind. Why, then, did he feel something was missing? He felt his cell vibrate in his pocket and retrieved it, glancing at the screen. It was a text from his life-long buddy, Tim.

*Drinks tonight? I'm buying.*

Daniel thought drinks and some intellectual conversation was exactly what he needed right now.

*I'm in, but I'm holding you to the treat. Julienne's at six?*

Tim replied: *You got it, partner. See you then.*

He glanced out the window, noticing the first hint of autumn as a few rogue leaves had fallen from their branches where they existed for the last six months. Another year, another step toward death. The view brought back a memory from almost forty years prior.

*Daniel steps outside into a world of intrigue. His young eyes soak up the carnival of colors. Gold and scarlet burst through the stubborn green which creates a symphony of hues and shades. His head falls back, and he looks skyward to the top of the giant trees which will seem to shrink in the future as he grows. He shields his eyes from the bright sunlight as a stiff breeze pushes his disheveled bangs back. A large bird takes flight from a towering oak tree, joining a family of others in a V formation. John tastes nature as he breathes in the crisp air. The season's first scent of a bonfire rides the wind. He is lost in the moment as he closes his eyes and savors the smell. His mind is free. His thoughts are clear.*

Daniel is snapped out of his spell as a motorcycle engine churns in the distance. He packs up his things and walks out of the lecture hall.

Daniel dropped his car off at home and called a cab to take him to Julienne's. He arrived early, grabbed a seat at the bar and ordered a scotch on the rocks. Julienne's was a comfortable upscale bar with nightly musical entertainment, usually in the form of a one-person outfit singing and playing acoustic guitar. Attached to the back of the bar was a pool hall with billiards, darts, and occasional poker tournaments. Daniel noticed two beauties at the end of the bar but quickly looked away, partly because they looked to be in their late twenties and partly because he thought it good practice. He had no desire or intention of ever cheating on Madison, so he thought it best just to stay out of situations that may tempt him. He knew of friends and colleagues who had started with a one-time mistake only for it to turn into a monthly occurrence. The door flew open and Tim walked in, glaring at the females as he strolled by.

"Daniel, great to see you. It's been what, a couple of months?"

"Six weeks or so," Daniel said as the two long-time friends shook hands.

"Not often enough, my friend. So, what's new? How's Madison? The kids?"

"Everything is perfect."

"Hey, you already ordered. It was supposed to be my treat."

"Started a tab, you can pick it up," Daniel replied with a smile. "So, what's new with you?"

"Well, blood pressure is still a tad high and my cholesterol needs attention, but those are trivial things."

"Trivial for now, maybe. But they can turn into major health problems. You have a perfect life, prolong it."

"That's rich coming from someone with a car beyond compare, a mansion for a house and a respected and fruitful career. You have the world by the balls, my friend," Tim said as he waved the bartender over and ordered a double martini.

"Hey, I know what kind of money stockbrokers rake in, and you have no family. Cha-ching. You must be rolling in it."

"I do okay."

"Just okay? What more do you want?"

Daniel noticed Tim's expression change slightly as he pondered the question. Tim was always a happy guy, living life to the fullest, no stranger to good times.

"Well, to be honest, I've kinda hit a rut in my life."

"Seriously? First I've heard of this. What seems to be the issue?"

"I'm bored."

"Bored? Bored of making huge money, dating beautiful women and living in a penthouse?"

Tim looked down as if ashamed of what he was about to say. "I know it seems ridiculous and I seem like a whiny bitch, but it's true. Is this all there is?"

Daniel quickly looked at Tim. That was the question he'd been asking himself frequently as of late. "You know, I feel the same way. Like life is passing me by and if I don't stop and look around a bit, I'll be an old man before I know it."

"Yes, like you're missing out on some secret of life?"

"Maybe, sure. But I'm married with children. You're still living the crazy bachelor life."

"It can be overrated. Don't get me wrong, getting a variety of women never gets old, but the grind does. I need to do something that pushes the boundaries that I'm used to. I need to involve myself in more fight or flight related experiences. When we live through those moments, like a first kiss, or in little league when we were up with the game on the line, time felt like it slowed to a halt. We can remember every little detail like it just happened, even thirty years later. Remember when I kissed Patty Dion on the lips the first time? I still remember the feel of her mouth, the taste, her soft tongue making contact with mine as it searched my mouth. Even today it sends a chill through me. How do we get that feeling back?"

"I wish I knew the answer. Time has flown by. The older we get, the more monotonous life becomes and the faster we age. Remember the summers in those days? They crawled by. They took an eternity. That's because as children everything we experience is fairly new. It isn't time that changes, time is always constant, it's how we perceive time that changes. Through the brain's processing of our senses, they get to experience and interpret the world and they use this perception to link moments of life into memories. Memories that are seared into our subconscious to return to us later in life."

"And those are the memories that seem to exist in eternity. The experiences that make us feel alive."

"Correct. When they happen, our senses are overloaded, fueled by the exposure to new experiences."

"So, how do we get that back?"

Daniel looked at his friend and shrugged. "I don't know."

Tim looked away toward the bartender, waving him over when he caught his attention.

"Another round?"

"Yes, please. Another double for me."

As the bartender walked to the other end of the bar to prepare their drinks Daniel continued. "Look, you've always lived on the edge. If either of us should know that answer, it would be you."

Tim watched as the two beauties at the end of the bar walked out. "I got an idea, but you have to agree to it and promise me you will follow through."

Daniel looked at Tim, wary of what his friend was going to ask of him. The bartender returned with their drinks.

"Thank you," Tim said, as the man walked away to the back room. "Daniel, we should make a pact. One weekend a month we go on an adventure. We can take turns choosing, but it has to be something that neither of us has ever done before."

"I don't know…"

"See that? Right there…that's why you feel dead. That's why you've lost your connection with your youth."

Daniel looked away, slowly shaking his head. "I have a wife, children…"

"So? You also have a life. Live it while you're still alive."

Daniel sipped his scotch while in deep thought. "It can't be anything against the law."

"Of course not."

"I have the right to veto anything you choose if it's...over the line."

"Over the line? What exactly does that mean?"

"Look, if you want me to agree to this, those are my terms."

"Okay, okay. You have veto power."

"I'll have to run it by Madison first."

"Of course. But if she agrees, you're in?"

Daniel extended his hand. "If she's cool with it, I'm in."

Tim grabbed his hand and pulled Daniel in for a hug. "That's my man!" Tim raised his glass in salute.

# Chapter Two

Daniel watched his wife undress until she wore only her matching black lace bra and panties. After all these years, witnessing her soft sexiness and her classic beauty still ignited his sexual desires in a way that other women simply could not. He dreaded discussing the plan he and Tim had agreed to. His wife was very understanding and grounded, but everyone had their insecurities that were triggered by just the right situation. Daniel didn't want any distrust between them, so he had to make her understand the reasons he wanted to do this.

"You look beautiful," he said as she reached for her pajama bottoms in her dresser drawer. She glanced up and acknowledged his compliment with a small smirk.

"Does this mean you want sex, or have something to tell me that I may not entirely like?"

Damn, he hated how well she knew him.

"No, it's just that you're still as beautiful as ever." This produced another glance, this time with no smile.

"Daniel, is there something you would like to discuss?"

"Yes."

"Well, why not just say that?"

"I was going to, but then I noticed how beautiful you are."

"Thank you. Now, what is it?"

"Well, you know I went to get a few drinks with Tim?"

"Yes, how is he? I haven't seen him in ages."

"Well, that's just it. He's kind of depressed."

"Depressed? Living the bachelor life, money, great job, dating anyone he wants, what's depressing about that?"

"Maybe depressed is a strong word," Daniel said carefully. "He's in a rut. He feels as if life is passing him by without knowing what it is he wants or needs."

"It sounds like just another way to say 'male-midlife-crisis.'"

"Okay, anyway, we were thinking, the first weekend of every month we'd go on an adventure. Do whatever sparks our interest, whatever we find enticing."

"The answer is yes," she said with no hesitation. "I know you've been down, I can feel it. I think it's a great idea and yes, you two should pursue whatever it is you need."

"Really? I mean, obviously, I'm happy with you, the kids, our life together. It's perfect, it's just, I need a diversion, something to push the boundaries again."

Madison curled up on the bed next to her husband. "Daniel, I love you. I want you to be as happy as possible. Go find your smile."

"Thank you, babe, I love you too." Moments later, his final thoughts before fading into a dream were how lucky he was to have Madison as his wife.

\* \* \*

That Saturday the Tigers football season opened with a noon-time home game against Harvard to kick off their season. Being not only a current professor but an alumnus and past member of the Princeton football team, Daniel attended every home game to support the them. He packed up a small grill along with food and drink into his pickup truck and waited for his family in the driveway. Having a few moments to kill, he called Tim.

"Hello, Daniel, give me some good news, my friend."

"Hey, Tim. I'm out. She said no way. There's too much that has to be done around the house and she wants to spend more time with me."

"Seriously? Dude, come on, man. I was looking forward to this."

"Just kidding. I'm in," Daniel said with a grin. "Gotcha, fuck face. That's for all the times you got me in trouble in school."

"Ha, well my friend, I was always a few steps ahead of you."

"Yeah, sure you were. So, the first weekend in October. Your choice—unless I veto your ass."

"Great! I'll do some research and let you know. Talk soon, Butch."

"Wait. Why the fuck am I Cassidy?"

"You know I'm always the Kid. That's non-negotiable."

Tim hung up before he could reply, leaving a smirk on Daniel's face. Tim had always been Daniel's best friend. Not only did the pair know how to have fun together, but they also had similar levels of intelligence, so discussing the more serious aspects of life came naturally to them. Daniel cherished their prolonged friendship and thought of Tim as the brother he never had.

The passenger door flew open and Daniel's family jumped into the truck. Daniel turned back to Logan who was seated behind him. "Did you remember the football, buddy?" Logan raised the football that Daniel had given to him for his last birthday. "Good boy. Remember, a tailgate isn't really a tailgate without throwing the pigskin around a bit."

Daniel pulled out of the driveway and headed for the highway, excited about the day ahead with his family and the weekends to come with his friend.

Daniel paced his classroom, stopping in front of his desk with his palms planted face-down on the beautifully patterned grain of the finished wood.

"When you look at me, what do you see?"

The students just looked at him, not understanding the question.

"Let's put Aristotle aside, I know today's lecture was scheduled to be about his legacy, but I have more pressing contemporary thoughts about life in general. So tell me, what do you see? Don't hesitate and for heaven's sake; don't worry about my feelings. Just say whatever comes to mind."

Susan raised her hand.

"Please, no hand raising, just say what comes to mind."

She put her hand down and said, "Wisdom."

"Wisdom, great, thank you. Anyone else?"

Suddenly, the students opened up.

"Intelligence."

"Kind of hot for a father figure," a young female blurted out, which brought laughter from the group.

"An older dude with a way with the ladies," Brian chimed in.

"Well, I'm flattered, but my time with the ladies is over. I'm a very happily married man. Anything else?" Nothing else came from the students. "Okay, the truth is, I may look like your father up here, lecturing you, feeding your minds with information I'm sure you all find to be trivial, but I'm just like all of you. I'm a college student wondering when the next party is, worrying about how I'm going to get through another set of finals, missing my family and the comforts of home. I'm a ten-year-old spending a summer afternoon swimming in a lake with my friends. I'm thirteen, encountering my first kiss, feeling the hair on my neck stand up from the electricity of the experience. I'm seventeen, falling in love for the first time, thinking my world revolves around those feelings. I was all those people just moments ago. Age isn't a disease, like cancer or polio. Our hearts remain the same as we age. Our passions remain the same. Sure, we gain wisdom, experience, and maturity, and our bodies begin to break down, but we'll always be children at heart."

Daniel paced the room, not even realizing he was moving. It created a potent, serious atmosphere that brought the students attention to full throttle. Teachers didn't usually talk like this.

"It is said that there are two kinds of sufferers in this world: Those who suffer from a lack of life, and those who suffer from an abundance of it. What do you think is meant by that statement?"

Julie, an introvert who usually abstains from joining in any type of discussion, raised her hand.

"Yes, Julie?"

"I think it means at times people go through the motions without living life to the fullest. Those are obviously the ones who suffer from lack of life."

"Okay, and the antithetical ones?" Daniel replied.

"Maybe that death is the ultimate equalizer. No matter how much we live life to the fullest or how much passion we have, someday we'll all die. The pinnacle, the realm of true spirit, will probably never be obtained."

"Very well stated, Julie. Yes, John?"

"Life is a balancing act, a fine line between having too much passion and not enough. Not enough and you live like a slug. Too much and you go insane."

"A balancing act indeed, another good explanation. Okay, great discussion today, class, but that's enough for today. We'll resume with Aristotle on Thursday."

* * *

The next few days dragged as Daniel anxiously awaited a call from Tim. He felt a reserved excitement growing inside as the first adventure was just under two weeks away. The family discussed his new plans over dinner one night.

"Uncle Tim and I will be going away the first weekend in October."

"Dad, Tim isn't really your brother, right? So why do we call him Uncle Tim?"

"No, he's not my brother, however, we've been friends for a long, long time. He's like a brother to me and an uncle to you two, so we'll call him Uncle Tim."

"Where are you going?" Logan asked.

"Well, I don't know yet. Tim is deciding."

"Isn't that scary?"

Daniel laughed. "No, actually it's kind of exciting, not knowing yet. It's almost like knowing you're getting a Christmas gift but having to wait until Christmas to open it."

"What if it's somewhere icky?"

"Icky? Where is icky?" Daniel said.

"Like a desert or the North Pole where you will freeze," said Logan, his age of six shining through.

"Wait a sec, the North Pole has Santa, how could that be icky?"

Logan just shrugged and went back to eating his lasagna.

"Seriously though, dad, what if you don't like what he picks?" Emily added.

"Well, I won't know that till I try it. I think everything will work out fine. I'll take pictures and we can talk every night and morning I'm away, deal?"

"Deal," his children said in unison.

"And you, my love, will be on my mind the whole time," he said as he grabbed Madison and pulled her onto his lap, finishing the gesture with a long kiss on the lips.

# Chapter Three

"Aristotle was and still is to this day considered the first 'scientist'. His understanding of logic, specifically induction and deduction have influenced the sciences and were used to create scientific theory. Logic was the fundamental tool which made learning and understanding possible, for it helped one to recognize when proof was needed and how to evaluate such proof. 'No great mind has ever existed without a touch of madness.' No truer words were ever spoken, for to create, one must break through the boundaries of what's considered the norm and take chances on abstract, sometimes even mad, thinking." Daniel glanced at the clock which read five before the hour. "That's a wrap for today, people. Enjoy your weekend and be safe."

After the room emptied, Daniel took out his cell to check his messages. There were a few from colleagues, discussing upcoming changes in the grading process. One from his dentist, confirming his appointment on Tuesday afternoon, and finally, one from Tim.

*Hey buddy, I have your fate in my hands and I've made a decision. Meet me at Julienne's at six.*

Daniel smirked and replied: *I'll be there.*

The rest of the afternoon crawled by as Daniel anticipated what Tim had planned for them. He arrived at Julienne's at five of six, Tim was already enjoying a drink at the bar.

"Hello Mr. Burton, your usual?" the bartender asked as Daniel sat next to Tim.

"Hi Tony, yes, thank you."

Tony turned away to pour his scotch.

"Well, fill me in. The suspense is crippling," Daniel said.

Tim reached into his back pocket, freeing a folded piece of paper and handed it to Daniel, who spread it out on the bar.

Daniel's eyes gazed upon the largest roller coaster he had ever seen.

"That, my friend, is The Monstrosity. The largest, fastest, highest roller coaster in the world. Twenty percent of people turn back and leave the line when they get closer to it. Twenty more vomit while riding it. We'll spend the weekend at the Paradox Park in Burbank, Illinois. There we will ride every ride, including The Monstrosity, at least once."

"Tim, you know I don't love coasters."

"That's why I picked this to start. Come on man, this is easy. The whole point is to step outside our comfort zones. You can do this."

Daniel sighed and raised his glass. "All right, it's on."

"That's my man. we're going to have a great time!"

"Aren't we a little too old for roller coasters?"

"Daniel, no one is too old for roller coasters."

\* \* \*

"Daddy, aren't you scared to go on that ride?" Emily asked her father as he tucked her in bed.

"Sure, but it's okay to be afraid at times. It's how you face your fears that matters. Usually, fears are built up in our own heads where they grow into these monsters that we can't face. In reality, the fear itself is worse than the actual cause of the fear."

"So, I shouldn't fear anything?"

"Well, fear is a natural warning to us that danger is close and we should be aware, but many times we create that same fear to grow to unrealistic levels. As you grow, you'll become better at recognizing the difference."

"Daddy, I'll miss you."

"Aww, I'll miss you too, sweetheart. But I'll only be gone for two days. I'll be back Sunday night in time to tuck you in. Now I have to say goodnight to your brother."

"Will I see you in the morning?"

"No, my flight is very early. You'll be asleep. Goodnight baby girl, Daddy loves you."

"Nite, Daddy."

Daniel walked into Logan's room. His son was reading a book which he drooped onto the floor when he saw his father walk in.

"Daddy!"

"Hi, buddy, whatcha' reading?" Logan was an avid reader, starting at the early age of five.

"Just a picture book."

"Yeah what's it about?"

"Max. He's a boy in a monster suit."

"Oh, the Wild Things. I remember reading that one as a child."

Logan turned his head to the side, seemingly confused by his father's statement.

"But, Dad, they had books back then?"

"Yes, Logan, they printed books when I was a young boy. What do you like most about it?"

"Definitely the different monsters."

"Yeah, me too."

"Daddy, when can I go on roller coasters with you?"

"Soon, son. Once you're old enough I'll take you. Aren't you afraid?"

"Nope, they are just coasters. I've seen videos of them online. Everyone seems to like it when they ride them."

"Okay, time for bed." Daniel tucked him in and patted his son on the shoulder. "You're a brave little man and I promise as soon as we can go, I'll take you on a coaster."

"Thanks, Dad!"

"Love you, son."

"Love you, too."

As he walked across the hallway and into his bedroom, Daniel flexed his left knee which he tore up playing high school football years ago. It had become arthritic over the years and would stiffen and become painful at times. He entered the bathroom, soaked a cloth in hot water, then wrapped it around the troublesome knee, instantly soothing the sharpness of the pain to a dull ache.

Lying in bed, Daniel thought about his six-year-old son's bravery and excitement towards exploring life and new experiences. If only he could regain that feeling. He dreamt of monsters and roller coasters.


The duo had a pleasant hour-and-a-half plane ride to Chicago Midway International Airport. An hour later they checked into their hotel rooms. Shortly after, they were in a rental car headed to Paradox Park.

"So, how are you feeling?" Tim asked as he dodged in and out of cars, which caused Daniel to double check his seat belt for security.

"I feel nervous but excited."

"See, that excitement. That's what we need more of. An unknown conclusion to an unfamiliar adventure."

Tim weaved past the last few cars and took the exit for Paradox Park. Moments later they were safely in the parking lot, through the gates, and walking the grounds. They walked up to the already growing line to ride The Monstrosity.

"You look like shit, dude. Don't worry, it'll be a piece of cake."

"Says the one who loves coasters," Daniel replied as he watched the frightening beast in action, going higher and faster than any ride before it. "This thing is fucking horrible."

Tim glanced at him and laughed. "You're going to be just fine, my man. Trust me."

Daniel felt the rush of fear take over his body. His palms started to sweat, his breathing quickened, increasing the oxygen supply to his brain and he felt his heart rate accelerate. As frightened as he was, there was a crystal clarity he experienced the closer he came to the actual ride. He felt every second, noticed every movement around him, heard every scream, cheer, and bout of laughter around him. Daniel made up his mind that no matter what, he'd stay the course and experience this crazy ride.

The coaster returned, the people were released with crazy, electric looks on their faces and Daniel thought: *This is what it's about, feeling that euphoria.*

The loading gate flew open and one by one the patrons were locked into their harnesses. Tim winked as they were separated and strapped in, with Tim directly in front of him. Time stood still as Daniel waited for the ride to begin. He could feel the buzz of the people around him; there was no turning back. His neck hairs peaked with anxiousness.

He jerked forward as the coaster started slowly and steadily. It reached a slow, climbing ascension and started its crawl into the sky. Daniel felt the flutter in his stomach and his blood pumping faster with every foot of the climb. Daniel closed his eyes, wishing it to be over quickly. Suddenly, the ascension leveled as they reached the pinnacle of the structure. There was a pause at the top, which would be forever branded into Daniel's mind. He opened his eyes and for the slightest moment felt a tranquil, inner peace as a soft breeze hit his face and he looked out for miles in every direction.

Then, all hell broke loose.

The rumble started as the people in front of him disappeared and the coaster picked up momentum. He heard the ear-piercing screams and suddenly he joined them, bellowing out as he headed straight down an incline of extreme length and degree. His adrenal glands were on full throttle, his body shook while he was taken through hoops, twists, turns, and a corkscrew. The excitement consumed Daniel as he felt every slingshot of velocity from every drop. The track finally straightened out and Daniel felt his body still in motion while his brain adjusted and the adrenaline still flowed. The ride came to a stop and Daniel felt like a ten-year-old again, his first thought in his mind: *I want to do it again. I want to do it five more times and feel like a kid again.*


Daniel arrived home on Sunday evening rejuvenated and refreshed. The truth was, Tim knew exactly what Daniel needed, and he thanked his friend before departing from the airport.

"So, how was the weekend?" his wife asked, as they lay together in an embrace.

"Madison, it was an awesome experience. I felt like a kid again. Once I got past my fear and my mind just accepting what was going to happen, my senses took over and welcomed every experience."

"Good, now you can take our children and go on all the rides with them, you know I hate coasters as well."

"Not 'as well', my dear, I now love them."

"Oh, really? I like this courageous, new version of you. Very sexy," she said, flashing her brilliant smile. Daniel grinned back and kissed her as he reached down and slid her panties off. He entered her and they made love, slowly and deliberately.

He woke and stumbled his way into the bathroom, catching a glimpse of his reflection in the mirror. As he paused to look at himself he was transported back to a moment from his past and his face seemed to grow younger.

*Daniel holds the popcorn container and soda as he glances over at Jessica, the pretty girl sitting next to him. She turns, catches his stare and smiles as if to say, "It's fine, you can look at me all you want." He quickly looks away as his face turns red. He is glad they chose 'home alone' as they laugh with each other at the funny little kid who seemingly gets the best of the tugs at every turn. Daniel places the containers on the floor and slowly puts his arm around her shoulders. He releases the breath he was unaware he was holding as her body seems to accept his touch. He glances at her once again and their eyes meet, and he takes a chance. He moves in and touches his lips to hers. He feels relief as her lips move to the contour of his, opening just a bit as he kisses her. He feels fireworks explode through his body and he feels alive; totally in the moment. It's everything a first kiss should be. Soft, gentle, and perfect.*

His lined face returned to his vision as the memory faded. Daniel turned away and continued to the bathroom before going back to bed.

# Chapter Four

"Do any of you play Monopoly?"

His students looked around at each other with no one answering.

"Come on, answer up, don't be shy. Raise your hand if you've played." Most of the classroom put their hands in the air.

"Okay, good. So, what property did you always try to obtain?"

Someone blurted out, "Mr. Burton, what does Monopoly have to do with philosophy?"

"Philosophy is, by definition, the study of the fundamental nature of knowledge, reality, and existence. Everything is philosophy. You just need to open your mind. Now, we can sit here, and I can continue to recite the classical philosophers, or we can discuss how philosophy can be used in our contemporary lives. So, which will it be?"

"Monopoly's cool," most of them accented.

"That's what I thought. Of course it's cool. It's the most popular board game of all time. Now, answer my question, please."

A few hands shot up.

"No hands, just say which properties you attempted to obtain every game."

"Boardwalk."

"Boardwalk."

"Park Place."

"Boardwalk."

The answers came in a flurry and all were either Boardwalk or Park Place.

"You people didn't win much, huh?"

The students looked around at each other.

"Everyone wanted Boardwalk and Park Place. Hell, I did as well when I first started playing the game. They were flashy, pricey, had stately names, and even were branded with the beautiful royal blue color. However, I am going to tell you which properties are best to own if you enjoy winning, and give you rational reasons why. The trio of St. James Place, Tennessee Avenue, and New York Avenue are the most revenue-generating properties on the board. Tabbed with an affordable price and houses that are relatively cheap, you can build up the trio quickly, whereas the prestigious side of the board requires more of an investment and more time to obtain the funds to invest. The orange properties are also located on the street where the jail is located, so you get all the convicts trespassing on your property as they leave prison. Just make sure you've installed a good security system."

Laugher came from the whole class and Daniel continued. "Also, the highest statistical outcomes of rolling two six-sided dice are as follows: six is 13.89%, 7 is 16.67%, 8 is 13,89%, and 9 is 11.11%. Well, would you believe when those dirty convicts leaving jail have three of the top four highest statistical chances of landing on the orange properties? On top of that, those prestigious green and royal blue properties have the go to jail space right before players turn onto their street, detouring many rent payments away from that street, to the street the actual jail is on."

Daniel looked around the room. Every one of his students was engaged, interested in the winning thought process.

"Fundamental nature of knowledge applied to the contemporary, real world of today. I've just taught you all how to use your brain to win the percentages of Monopoly games you play for the rest of your lives. My students and friends, that *is* philosophy."

The class ended and Daniel watched the students exit that day, hoping they all left with a better understanding and appreciation of just what philosophy was and meant to the existing world around them.


Daniel immediately started brainstorming for the duo's next adventure. He thought about past experiences that made him feel young, alive, and free. He remembered the first concert he saw while in college with his current girlfriend, Stacy. He and Tim's favorite band, Tool, played in Holmdel N.J. in 1998 at the PNC Bank Arts Center, which Stacy agreed to attend. Tim had wanted to go as well, but circumstances at the time prevented his presence. The circumstance being a girl Tim was seeing at the time had thought she was pregnant, and Tim wasn't in the mood to party. It turned out Tim wasn't about to become a father, but he always regretted missing the concert. Daniel remembered the experience like it happened yesterday. Knowing Tool was on tour this year, he searched the upcoming dates and venues. The first weekend in November they'd be at a cozy little venue in Savannah, Georgia, called The Stage on Bay. The small venue was uniquely configured to present arena-style shows in the intimacy of a theater-club setting. It was a special show they were putting on for the people of Savanah to celebrate

Halloween. Savanah was the oldest town in Georgia and is also considered by many to be the spookiest place in America.

*This is perfect* he thought. If only he could obtain tickets for the show. Every ticket vendor he checked was sold out, so he searched consumer online marketplaces and got a hit. A couple were selling a pair of tickets to the show for a thousand dollars each. Daniel sighed. Two thousand dollars, for a concert? Just as he was about to leave the page, he froze. *This is exactly what I need to do. It's only money, but the experience is priceless.* He clicked on the 'buy now' tab, and the money was transferred from his online account. He entered his address and received an email saying, 'Congrats, your tickets are on their way!' Daniel sat back in his chair and smiled, knowing a month ago he wouldn't have gone through with the purchase.

"Daniel, I think it's a fabulous idea. Where will you stay?" Madison asked with her head comfortably placed on Daniel's chest. They'd just made love and were now basking in the afterglow.

"Well, that's the brilliant part of the trip. Savannah is known as the most mysterious, eerie town in America. I'll reserve a night at each of their most haunted inns. Ghosts freak Tim out, and it just so happens I owe him one for the coaster trip."

"It sounds like a wonderful weekend, my dear."

Daniel glanced at his wife. "Do I sense a bit of sarcasm?"

"Well, it's just…" Madison paused and bit her lip. "You've never put this much effort into our time together."

"But that's just it! I'm changing. I promise you the next trip we take I'll spare no expense and you won't have to do a thing. I'll plan everything."

Madison smiled. "Sounds great, but, when?"

Daniel hugged her and kissed the top of her head, inhaling her delicious, natural scent. "As soon as this *experiment* is over."

"How long will that be?"

"Come on honey, you know I'm a philosophy professor. It's up to the gods, not men."

# Chapter Five

"Arthur Schopenhauer, the German philosopher from Danzig, Poland, is known as the philosopher of pessimism, articulating a worldview that challenges the value of existence. He contended that at its core, the universe is an irrational place and that we should minimize our natural desires for the sake of achieving a more tranquil frame of mind and a disposition towards universal beneficence."

Daniel paused and glanced around the room to see if he still had the attention of his students. He then walked to the chalkboard and wrote out a sentence book-cased by quotes. "His quote: 'The two enemies of human happiness are pain and boredom,' has been examined, studied, scrutinized, and debated over. Just what did he mean by these words? You're all looking at me with a confused look on your faces. Maybe that's the point. Maybe their meaning was meant to be different for everyone.

"Class, we'll take a quick break for you to read them over again and contemplate what your own thoughts about these words are."

Daniel walked out of the classroom and stepped outside to get a breath of fresh air. The brilliant sun shone down on his face and he felt every ray. Birds chirped, a slight breeze pushed his hair back off his forehead, and he closed his eyes, experiencing every detail of the fine day. He was alive, living in this moment, putting yesterday and tomorrow aside and all the stress and tension that comes with them. He smiled, glanced around him one last time and turned to walk back to his class.

He re-entered his classroom to a wave of discussion about pain and boredom.

"Quiet, please. Now, who'd like to voice their opinion of Schopenhauer's quote?"

A few hands were raised.

"Yes, Susan?"

"I think he meant emotional pain, which can paralyze people's desire to do anything, which leads to boredom."

"Very good. Anyone else?" Tom Mueller raised his hand. "Yes, Tom?"

"I agree with Susan. I think the two are linked. Boredom causes pain and pain causes boredom because it stunts our passion."

"Okay, anyone else?" Julie, who before had hardly ever raised her hand in any class for any reason, once again chose to participate for the second time in the last three lectures. Daniel nodded in her direction. "Julie? Go ahead."

"For me, it reflects the paradox we live by. As Susan and Tom implied, we are inundated with pain, which is an automatic and daily part of life, which subsequently saps our desires and passions to live. That's why when couples have stress in their lives, they have less sex."

"I think I'm in love," Brain said as he took in Julie's words. "A hot, quiet woman with a brain can be very sexy." The room broke out in laughter. Daniel put up his hand to regain order.

"Excellent, Julie. I won't give you my personal opinion of his quote because I want you all to decide for yourselves, but I'll say what I've heard so far is great thinking and that's what I strive to get from all of you—thought. That's all for today, have a great weekend and be safe."

Daniel chuckled to himself as he watched Brian chase Julie down the hall. *Sex, to be young and carnal. Schopenhauer was right, without passion and desire we bore and sag, spiritually, emotionally, and physically.* Daniel smiled and walked out of the classroom with pure, youthful thoughts filling his mind.

Daniel walked into Julienne's noticing Tim already present at the bar. He sat next to his friend and smiled.

"Are you ready for this?"

"First we have to get a drink in you, and a second drink in me."

Tim ordered a round and when the drinks came he turned to Daniel. "Okay, shoot."

"Do you remember in college when we had the chance to see Tool in Jersey? You couldn't go at the time because, well...let's just say your little weenie got you into some trouble."

"Please don't remind me. I still have nightmares about that."

"Well, I know you haven't seen them since, so, we're about to spend the weekend in the most haunted town in America and see our favorite band."

"No shit? Dude, that's awesome. Where?"

"Savannah, Georgia. The stage on Bay."

"How the fuck did you pull that off? That's a cozy venue, must have cost a fortune."

"Well, yeah, kinda. But that's just the start. We're spending each night in the two most haunted inns in the country."

"Fuck, man. You know ghosts freak me out."

"Just like coasters do me."

"Okay, I get your point. I'm in."

"Of course you're in, only I have veto power." Daniel raised his glass. "To Savannah, and Tool."

Tim smiled, "To Savannah, and Tool."


Days passed and suddenly it was Thursday, the eve of the Savannah trip. After Daniel put the children to bed, he and Madison made love like they were sixteen again, full of life and passion. Madison placed her head on his chest as the couple basked in the afterglow.

"Wow, that brings back memories of our first year together. If this is what these trips are going to do to you, you have my blessing to go on as many as you'd like."

Daniel kissed her and held her tight. "It's not just the trips, I realize I love you more than ever and I want you to feel that from me."

"Oh, I do. So, are you excited for tomorrow?"

"Tool's great, but I'm really looking forward to seeing Tim getting the shit scared out of him."

"What are best friends for? I'll miss you."

Daniel held her body to his. "I'll miss you more."

The couple faded into a deep sleep together, Daniel's heart was filled with love for her.


On Friday evening, the duo flew into the Savannah Hilton Head Airport and less than an hour later checked into the Hamilton-Turner Inn located in the center of the historic district of Savannah. A stunning, stately, southern, Victorian mansion, the elegant structure exuded history at every turn. Daniel picked up a pamphlet at the front desk as they passed through to their room. It told of the historical stories which led to the claimed paranormal activities that had transpired through the years. He placed the pamphlet in his back pocket thinking it would make excellent reading for Tim later that evening.

After dinner, they returned to the inn and retired to their room for the night. Daniel remembered the pamphlet he'd stored away in his back pocket and opened it as Tim settled in and welcomed sleep.

"Tim, listen to these stories about the history of this place. The original owner, Samuel P. Hamilton, owned a museum-quality art collection, which he employed a hired gun to guard. This hired gun would patrol from atop the roof nightly. One evening, he didn't complete his duty and was found murdered by gunshot to the back of his head. Nothing was stolen and the crime was never solved. It's said the guard's ghost to this day patrols the roof with the same Springfield model rifle he carried when he was alive."

"Brilliant. I'll be sure to wave when I see him up there."

"Here's another. In 1915, Doctor Francis Turner purchased the mansion to serve as both his home and practice which he set up in the basement. The Turner's would throw extravagant parties in their home. Unfortunately, those parties came to a sudden tragic halt due to the accidental death of the doctor's daughter. During these parties the children were banished upstairs where they'd play with the balls on the billiard table. One night, the children rolled balls down the stairs so they could retrieve them and catch a glimpse of what the adults were up to. One of the little girls, the doctor's daughter, got too close to the top step and fell down the stairs to her death. Her ghost is rumored to still roll billiard balls throughout the inn once night falls."

Tim looked at Daniel. "Go fuck yourself."

Daniel doubled over in laughter. "What dude? I'm just filling you in on some of the history."

Tim got in bed and rolled over. "Shut off the damn light."

"Wait, there are a few more. A Civil War soldier apparently wandering the halls, knocking on doors, due to the structure being built upon his grave. Phantom footsteps cascading down the hall at all hours of the night and a cigar smoking specter, seen all over the grounds, thought to be Samuel Hamilton himself, keeping watch over his former home."

"I'm going to sleep. Goodnight."

Daniel laughed, placed the pamphlet on the night-stand and reached over to click the lamp off. "Goodnight, buddy. Ignore the sounds, they'll just be your imagination."


Daniel woke to Tim's pleading.

"Daniel are you awake? I keep hearing footsteps in the hallway."

Daniel glanced at the bed-side clock. "It's 3:00. Go back to sleep."

"No, seriously, go check it out."

"Why me?"

"Wait, listen."

Daniel got up, walked to the door and put his ear against the wood. What he heard sent chills down his spine. Slow, deliberate footsteps coming from the end of the hallway. Too slow to be an actual person. Too deliberate to be the gait of someone out for a late stroll.

"Holy shit, dude."

"What the fuck is it? Go check."

"Why me, you coward?"

"You brought us here. It was your idea. You need to go check it out."

"Why don't we just go back to sleep? The steps obviously aren't meant to do us any harm."

"How do we know that?"

"Because they haven't tried to get into our room yet."

"Yet? Maybe you can accept yet. You seem to like ghosts. I on the other hand, despise the whole concept."

Suddenly the steps ceased exactly in front of their door.

"Daniel, what the fuck!" Tim whispered.

Daniel reached for the doorknob.

"Wait, don't," Tim whispered hoarsely.

Daniel put a finger up towards his frightened friend. Slowly he turned the knob and eased the door open. Tim pulled the covers over his head. Daniel stepped into the hall. He appeared moments later. "Nothing."

"How the fuck can it be nothing? We both heard it."

"How the hell should I know, but there's nothing there now so obviously whatever *it* was, meant us no harm. I'm going back to bed." Daniel closed the door, locked it behind him, and climbed back into bed.

There was silence for a couple of minutes until Tim spoke. "Daniel, can I get in your bed?"

"*What*? Go to sleep, you chicken-shit pansy."

The last thing Daniel heard before fading away to neverland was Tim whispering, "Thanks a lot."

# Chapter Six

Daniel woke early to Tim clamoring about the room. Knowing getting more sleep would be a futile effort, he got up and headed to the bathroom to shower before going down for breakfast.

"Damn, you look like shit," Daniel said as he glanced at Tim who had turned on the television now that Daniel was awake.

"Yeah, well, I hardly slept. Those footsteps continued all night."

"Well, tonight we're staying in a different inn called The Marshall House."

"Another haunted structure?"

"Tim, everything in this town is rumored to be haunted."

"Great, what a wonderful vacation."

"Hey, Tool is tonight. There'll be no phantoms there, just intense, loud, live music."

"Thank the heavens. I need a fucking break."

They ate breakfast and spent the day touring the town. At nightfall, they checked into The Marshall House and headed to the concert venue, leaving plenty of time for slow traffic. Minutes later they were seated in the tenth row, center aisle. The crowd buzzed as the start of the concert grew near. The setting at this venue was more intimate than what the normal Tool concert was, which Daniel thought only added to the charm and importance of the trip. The entire theater was blanketed in darkness except for behind the stage, which was backed by a monolithic, laser shooting LED screen that donned TOOL in giant red letters, backed by what looked like continuous pouring black smoke.

Soon the music started with the warm crunch of the guitars, the dark dropped tone of the bass and the thick 70's sound of the drums. The small venue came to life and suddenly seemed like an arena with fifty-thousand screaming fans all pumping their fists to the beat of the music. Daniel turned to glance at Tim who was wide eyed and taking in the live music that evaded him so many years ago. With draft beers in hand, by mid concert the duo could have passed for college students living life to the fullest with no responsibilities but to enjoy this night. The lights and laser show were sights to see as the progressive rock music played on through an encore. When the show was over, they headed to the hotel, euphoric and rejuvenated, feeling like a couple of teenagers, their senses filled with the sights and sounds of the best concert they'd ever seen.

Daniel was glad their stay at The Marshall House went without any interruptions of hauntings of the like that had occurred at The Hamilton-Turner Inn. They finished the weekend with an early dinner before flying back home Sunday evening. Daniel walked into a quiet house with the children already in bed.

"Look at that smile. I take it you had a nice weekend?" Madison asked as Daniel took her in his arms.

"I missed you. Everything was absolutely perfect. The concert was something we'll remember for the rest of our lives, although Tim was scared shitless on Friday night at the Hamilton-Turner Inn."

"Why, is it really haunted?"

Daniel held her face in his hands and glanced up at the ceiling before replying. "You know, I actually think it is."

"You know I don't believe in ghosts."

"Neither do I, or maybe I should say neither *did* I."

Madison smiled and led him by the hand into their bedroom.

"Hold on, I want to check on them first," Daniel said as he headed out of the bedroom. "Hold that thought."

After checking on Logan, he entered Emily's room. Het sat down beside her bed to watch her sleep. It seemed just yesterday she was a baby, now her future teenage years waiting in the wings. He felt a short stab of pain in his heart as he realized those moments are forever gone, never to return. He wondered why we don't realize at the time how important each moment that becomes a memory is, and how many times our minds will search them out for the rest of our lives. What would he give to change one more diaper with his daughter smiling back at him, as if they were playing a game? How much were the early Saturday mornings alone with Emily worth now? What would it be worth to re-live just one more?

Small tears rolled from his eyes as he watched his innocent daughter sleep, the memory of that day in the delivery room when he looked at her for the first time and saw his owns eyes look straight back at him, fixed in his mind. He wiped his eyes and returned to his bedroom and made love to his wife like they'd been apart for a decade.


"Every life...mine, yours, your friends, your relatives, is consisted of a network of choices, each one sending us off towards another decision, another fork in the road. Should we turn left...right? Go straight? The universe is in flux. It expands, then contracts, creating an infinite number of scenarios and outcomes, each creating a new set of choices. Or, maybe we shouldn't decide at all and let fate take the wheel. Does anyone here play chess?" One or two hands went into the air. "Great, have you heard of the term zugzwang?" Laughter ensued. "Okay, okay, yes it's a strange sounding word, but its meaning is very interesting; it refers to a situation found in the game wherein one player is put to a disadvantage because they must make a move when the best decision for the outcome of their game is not to move. The move will make their position significantly weaker. By comparison, the same theory can be used in life, as long as you don't choose, anything is possible.

"The difference is, because time being temporal, not metaphysical or spiritual, and the physics of time being forward movement only, we don't realize it. In the end, maybe our choices don't matter as much as we seem to think they do. Maybe there's a simpler choice, one not driven by chaos or rational certainty. Maybe we just simply choose to be happy, whatever the circumstance. Life is here, now, in this moment. Capture and experience it all and live it to the fullest."

Daniel looked up at the faces of his students, all in deep thought and attentive to what he was lecturing. *Tis is why I do it,* he thought. *To see my words sink into their brains. To make a difference in their lives, to help them grow, think, and mature.*

The following weekend Daniel took the family to the Camp May County Zoo. It was an unseasonably warm November day with temperatures in the low fifties. He watched his children as they enjoyed themselves without reserve or regret. They were *living*, not just alive, as if that trait was something only children could obtain. He watched his daughter laugh while watching the camels and witnessed his son smile and dance as he gazed upon his favorite animal, the lion.

He witnessed the pure joy of youth, which was something he was sure was always there, but he really hadn't noticed before.

"Dad, look at the lion!"

"I know, son. He's beautiful."

"Dad, he's not beautiful, he's awesome!"

"He is!"

"Why is he considered the king?"

Daniel studied the beast laying in the shade, as he blinked at the boring humans as they pointed, waved, and showed their excitement of viewing him. The beautiful golden hue of his mane glittered when the sunlight cascaded down upon it. He was truly a majestic beast, something so gorgeous, yet so dangerous, passive yet aggressive, tranquil yet vicious, that it was truly an awesome sight to behold.

"Well, I think it's partly because of his appearance. Just look at that mane. It's royalty, is it not? He also has no fear. He lives in the plains and wide-open areas as opposed to other animals that hide in their habitat. Also, he protects the pride to his death and his roar can be heard for miles. No other animal can make that distinct of a sound or travels nearly as far."

They passed the Black Bears, Snow Leopards and Silver Foxes, and approached the primates. Daniel paused in front of the monkeys.

"Dad, they move just like us," Emily said. "I learned that we're related to them in science class the other day."

Daniel noticed the way they held their young, their facial expressions and obvious intelligence.

"Emily, there are different thoughts on how humans came about on earth. What you learn in church will vary significantly from what you will learn in school."

She glanced at her father with a confused expression. "Which should I believe?"

"That's for you to determine, sweetie. Be aware of all the different beliefs then decide which you think is right for you."

Daniel continued to study the monkeys and he couldn't help but wonder which school of thought he believed in—evolution or creative design. If he, a philosophy professor seasoned through years of study couldn't determine which side he believed in, how could a child? But maybe that was the point. Maybe humans need to somehow believe in both.

The following week Daniel was between lectures when he received a text from Tim:

*Drinks at Julienne's at six. I have our next adventure.*

Daniel replied: *I'll be there.*

For the rest of the school day he wondered what Tim had picked and the anticipation grew as the six o'clock hour grew near. After correcting exams and reviewing his next lecture, he headed to Julienne's. When he walked in Tim already on his second drink.

"Hello, partner," he said as he took a seat at the bar next to his friend.

Tim quickly looks up from the liquid gold in his glass. "Daniel, I didn't see you arrive. How was school?"

"It was an interesting lecture today. We discussed mortality and the inevitable end that awaits us all."

"Sounds enthralling. Do you give out suicide hotline numbers after class?"

Daniel couldn't help the short burst of laughter that came out, he said, "No. Philosophy can be many things, and depressing is included in that spectrum. Suffice to say, I could use a little uplifting news."

"I'm getting to that, don't worry. Let's get you a drink first."

"Sure, the usual."

Tim ordered the round and turned back to Daniel. "Have you ever heard of ziplining?"

"You mean flying around the woods attached to a harness? That ziplining?"

"Well, sure. However, it can be much more extreme than that. There's a place in the White Mountains of New Hampshire called Alpine Adventures. They've just opened a Super Sky-rider ziplining tour with the longest, fastest, highest lines in the country."

"How long, how fast, and how high are we talking here?" Daniel said after downing a mouthful of scotch.

Tim smiled. "Two-thousand feet long, seventy miles per hour, and...well, it can be up to three hundred feet off the ground."

Daniel stared at Tim a moment. "What? Are you shitting me?"

"No, trust me, you'll love it. I've been there before and it's a super rush."

"Have you been to this *extreme* one?"

"No, but I can't wait. I booked the first weekend in December so there will be snow on the mountains. It will be beautiful."

Daniel took another gulp of scotch. "Okay, anything I should bring?"

"Just your courage."

Daniel gave Tim a frown as he finished off his drink.


On the ride home, a song came on the radio that immediately transported him to another time.

*Daniel watches as the setting sun shines off his black '86 Cutlass Supreme*

*He had worked in a restaurant for two years to save up the money to buy his first car and as he stands in his driveway watching his father screw on his new license, he feels a burst of pride and accomplishment.*

*His father glances up at him before he stands and smiles.*

*"All set, son. Take her for a spin."*

*He feels the thin, plastic square in his jacket pocket as he slides into the driver's seat, turns the key, and hears the six-cylinder, 3.8 litre engine come to life. Before he backs out, he removes the object from his pocket. He holds it in his hand as he studies the cover. It's obsidian black with a cross sporting five skull heads all decorated with different hats, glasses, and handkerchiefs. He pops the round disc out and inserts it into the slot on the radio. He is so excited to be the first of his friends to own a vehicle with a CD player. As he slowly backs out, the insane guitar intro assaults the speakers as his mother joins his father in watching their son drive his own car for the first time. By the time he is heading down his street, the song is in full force as the singer's piecing scream comes to an end and the full band kicks in. He holds his head high as pride flows form his pores. He would remember this moment for the rest of his life as the first time he felt like a man and in control of his own world; his own destiny. Though it's a brisk fifty-five degrees out, he rolls down the window and cranks the music.*

'Welcome to the Jungle' ends just as Daniel pulls into the driveway. He remains seated as he kills the engine and the flashback dissolves from his mind. He closes his eyes to try to regain the feeling once again, but it was gone. He pulls the keys from the ignition and heads inside.

"Ziplining, huh? Sounds exhilarating."

"It's not just ziplining, it's *extreme* ziplining."

"Are you sure you're ready for this? I mean it must be quite a bit of climbing involved," Madison said with a smirk on her face.

"Hey, I've lost a couple pounds in the last two months. Haven't you noticed? I feel like I have more energy."

"Yes, dear, you look like a lean teenager."

"I'm serious. I actually feel better since we started this pact."

"Well, I've noticed you found your smile. Why don't you invite Tim over for Thanksgiving dinner?"

"That's a great idea. The kids haven't seen him in a while, and I know he has no where to go. His parents are on the west coast and he has no steady girlfriend."

"It's settled then, invite him and I'll set an extra place at the table."

# Chapter Seven

"Lies. We all tell lies. Sixty percent of the population can't go ten minutes without lying, according to studies done by psychologists. A whopping twenty percent of everything said is either a lie, or a slightly twisted version of the truth. However, I'm here today to tell you that lies are a complicated entity and there are many varying degrees and versions."

Daniel paused to let that last sentence sink in and to look over his students. He noticed Julie in the back of the room with her head down and her right hand over her left arm. "Immanuel Kant, an eighteenth century Prussian philosopher, claimed that lying is wrong. No matter what. He implored that the duty to not lie must *always* be more important than any conflicting duty. Who here today agrees with Mr. Kant?" Half of the students raised their hands. "Susan, let's expand on this. Do you believe it's morally sound and to always tell the truth?"

"Sure, I mean honesty is always the best policy, right?"

"Damn, girl, you sound like Kant himself." The class roared in laughter.

"Susan, do you intend to have children?"

"Yes, of course."

"Will you celebrate Christmas? Easter?"

"Sure, if my significant other shares the same beliefs."

"Okay, will you tell your children the story of Santa Clause and how he'll travel the globe in one night, spreading gifts to all? Will you place Easter eggs in your yard seemingly placed there by a fictional rabbit who you'll tell your children is real? Will you tell them to place their discarded teeth under their pillows and replace them with money seemingly from a pretty fairy who flies around with beautiful butterfly wings?" Daniel waved his arms up and down to illustrate fairy wings, bringing another round of laughter.

"Well, yes, but that's different."

"Why is it different? They're lies, and they're just the start. You see, they're what we refer to as 'little white lies' to bring others happiness, or in this case, to let small children believe in magic while they're young and innocent before this world brings them to their knees. All the same, they're lies. Guys, have you had girlfriends who ask you, 'Do these jeans make me look fat?'"

All the boys raised their hands in unison, laughing and high fiving each other.

"I see, and how many of you tell the truth?" All the hands went down. "See, that's self-preservation. Surly not the most morally sound way to handle the situation but required if you wanted to remain alive. Now, I agree there are lies that are only self-serving which can end up hurting others, and surely these lies should be extinguished, yet we must police ourselves and make those decisions in our own minds and hearts. Ask yourselves this question—what kind of person do I really want to be?"

The class ended and when Julie walked by, Daniel noticed a bruise on her upper arm in the form of a handprint. Before he could react, she was gone. Minutes later with his lectures for the day complete, Daniel filed away his paperwork in his case and headed down the hallway. As he turned into the stairwell heading into the parking lot he came across Brian, pushing a fellow student down the stairs.

"Brian, what the hell are you doing!"

Brain turned with rage in his eyes. "Mr. Burton, he's Julie's boyfriend and he hits her. Grabs her by the arm, leaving bruises. I was telling him he better stop it. He turned and swung at me, so I pushed him."

"Bullshit!" the other boy said. "He came after me and pushed me from behind. I'm going to the principal!" The boy took off down the stairs with blood oozing from his elbow and upper arms.

Daniel walked Brian to the principal's office where the boy was receiving medical attention from the nurse. They walked in and sat across from Principal Hawkings.

"Now, what's your side of the story, son? What Michael presumes happened between you and Julie is a very serious matter."

Brian said, "Mr. Hawk, I—"

Daniel held his hand up. "Silence. I'll explain this. You've done enough already. Peter, I saw it all. They were wrestling with each other when Michael lost his balance and lost his footing. Brian didn't push him. Now, surely both should be reprimanded for the horseplay in school, but it's hardly as serious a matter as Michael wanted you to believe"

"Very well. You both will receive ten hours of community service. I'm now watching you, Mr. Harris. You best be on your top behavior."

Daniel and Brian walked out together. When they reached the courtyard, Brian turned to Daniel. "Thank you, Mr. Burton. What he does to her is wrong."

"Of course it is, and I'll take care of it, but however brave and virtuous your actions were, it's not your place."

"I know and thank you for lying for me."

"Hey, I never liked Kant. He's a blowhard."

Brian nodded his head and smiled before continuing on his way.


The following day Daniel asked Julie to speak to him after class. She waited in her seat as the classroom emptied. When they were alone, Daniel sat in the seat next to her.

"Julie, I know Michael hurts you. I've seen the bruises. We need to put a stop to this by contacting the authorities."

Julie dropped her head and put her hand over her face. When she looked up tears were falling freely down her cheeks.

"Mr. Burton, please. He doesn't mean it. He loses his temper sometimes."

"You deserve better, Julie. If you want to be treated better, you must *demand* to be treated better. Take control of the situation, break up with him or I'll step in and solve it my own way."

"If I break up with him, he'll be enraged. I'm afraid of what he'll do."

Daniel got up and paced the classroom. He knew this was a delicate situation and wanted to help her without putting her in physical danger.

"I'm going to talk to him. You'll be safe, trust me."

Julie's eyes dropped. Concern and despondency overtook her.

"Everything will be fine, Julie."

A forced hint of a smile appeared as her eyes met Daniels. "Please be careful, Mr. Burton."

# Chapter Eight

T hanksgiving Day arrived, bringing cold temperatures with it. Flurries fell as Daniel, Tim, Emily, and Logan went outside to throw the football around while Madison prepared the food. The Burton's did the typical Thanksgiving dinner with turkey, stuffing, cranberry sauce, and all the trimmings. When the food was ready, everyone came inside to eat and then watch the football games. Tim and Daniel settled in each with a piece of pumpkin pie as the second game kicked off.

"So, are you ready? Next weekend will come quickly," Tim said.

"I'm actually looking forward to it. You know, the more you push the boundaries and try things that take you out of your comfort zone, the more you enjoy it. It's almost addictive."

"It *is* addictive, your body releases a hormone called epinephrine which makes your heart race faster, increases blood flow to the brain, and stimulates your whole body. Your whole system pretty much gets high without the use of illegal narcotics," Tim said with a smile.

"How the hell do you know all of this?"

"I've been studying up on it just to educate myself. Daniel, I really think we've stumbled onto something here that will change our lives for the better."

Daniel's attention returned to the television as the Cowboys scored the first touchdown of the game. He turned away in disgust. Being a Giants fan meant instinctively rooting against the Cowboys.

With the conclusion of the second game, Tim thanked Madison for the delicious food, hugged the children and headed home. Daniel put the kids to bed and then crawled in next to Madison.

"Thank you for dinner, babe. Everything was perfect. Tim really enjoyed himself."

"I'm glad. He seems...different. Less stressed, more alive."

"Well, that's the point of our pact. To make our bodies and minds feel alive again. Speaking of feeling alive..."

Daniel pulled off her clothes like he was sixteen and on a date with his first girlfriend again. They made love passionately like it was the last time they would be together.

Afterwards, Madison fell asleep with her head on Daniel's chest and his mind drifted back to a time before Madison; before their children and their life together.

*Daniel spreads the blanket out on the fine golden sand as the sun relents its reign over the world and starts its decent behind them to the west. The waves violently yet hypnotically crash onto the shore and the moon shows its glowing face for the first time over the Atlantic.*

*"Its absolutely beautiful," his date says, as they take in the developing scene. Her name is Joy, and she is perfect. As perfect as a first steady girlfriend could be at seventeen. Her honeysuckle, blonde hair glows in the steadily growing moonlight and Daniel captures her blue eyes flash when she turns to smile at him. It's the day after the*

*prom and the couple refused to make love on that Friday night to avoid being a cliché. They'd agreed on dinner the following evening with plans to consummate the relationship. Daniel feels his heart race as he reaches to Joy's face to prevent a few strands of golden hair from assaulting her beautiful eyes. He feels alive, unlike ever before. Every aspect of the evening is super defined and evident to his senses. The scent of the ocean, the feel of the soft breeze soothing them, the bright glow of the moonlight reflecting off the azure water. It is a perfect scene, alone on a beautiful beach with nothing but nature. Daniel smiles at Joy, closes his eyes and lowers his head to kiss her lips. He feels the excitement and adrenaline as they become one. He pauses the moment before he enters her body to look into her eyes. It is a moment he knows he will remember for the rest of his life. What will it feel like? Will we both enjoy it? Will I be good enough? He closes his eyes and feels her warmth as he slowly enters...*

He ran his fingers over the back of Madison's head, feeling her soft hair under his touch. The memory returned to him every now and again, so familiar, so real. He loves Madison deeply and wouldn't change their life together for anything, but that memory was part of him, part of who he had become. It was as much a part of him as his body and soul were. He closed his eyes to relive it one more time before falling asleep next to his wife.


"Today, my philosophical disciples, I'd like to plug in those brilliant, young minds and see what kind of magic they can produce. Does anyone here enjoy riddles?" This was the final lecture of the day, so Daniel planned to make it interesting and different, as textbook study waned the closer to the end of the day it became.

Daniel looked over his students who glanced at each other and back at their crazy professor.

"Seriously, no one here enjoys a good riddle every now and then? I love them. I love to figure out problems using just my brain. I believe as humans we are programmed to uncover solutions to problems and explanations to riddles. We have an instinctive nature to absorb knowledge." Daniel paused to glance around the classroom at the scowls and sneers on the faces of the world's best and brightest. "Cheer up, homosapiens, you're all given those huge melon brains for a reason, and playing Fortnight wasn't it."

Groans filled the room.

"The first ingenious student who can give me the correct answer will receive an extra ten points on their next test."

This announcement brought full attention to the riddle in question. Daniel inwardly grinned as he watched the students all sit up straight and concentrate on every word now that there was something to be gained.

"Ah, that's what I like to see. The desire to achieve if we are compensated properly. That's what capitalism is based on, and we are a capitalistic society." Daniel turned to the chalkboard to scrawl the riddle:

There are three boxes, one contains only apples, one contains only oranges, and one contains both apples and oranges. These boxes have been incorrectly labeled such that no label identifies the actual contents of the box it labels. Opening just one box, and without looking in it, you can take out one piece of fruit. By looking at the fruit, how can you immediately label all the boxes correctly?

Daniel placed the chalk on his desk. "I'll give you the rest of this period, young geniuses. Your treasure awaits."

With that, he walked out of the room, leaving his students to decipher the riddle. He headed down the hall and outside into the courtyard. Steely grey clouds assaulted the sky and the late November wind kicked up, hitting Daniel in the face with a crisp, refreshing sensation. He reflected on the upcoming weekend and gliding through the tree-tops of the White Mountains. His thoughts created a child-like excitement as he continued his walk around the courtyard.

Exercising was something he promised himself to engage in more often and walking daily around the school courtyard was a solid start. A high sun threatening to break through the thick cloud cover to the east as the wind kicked up again blowing his hair straight back. After the formidable stroll, he returned to the classroom eager to learn of the progress his students made.

"Well, do we have any guesses? Anyone?"

Julie stood and spoke. "We have a guess, however, we talked through it together and came to this conclusion together."

Daniel was proud of his introverted student. When she attended his first lecture, she never raised a hand and talked only when spoken too. She had slowly showed more confidence and had become a vocal leader of the class. This transformation gave Daniel a glowing, warm feeling inside.

"Okay, well, let's hear it."

"You must pick a fruit from the box labeled with both apples and oranges."

Daniel smiled at the clever minds of his students.

"Yes, you're correct. Would you like to give an explanation as to why, Julie?"

"The key to the riddle is 'all three boxes are labeled incorrectly'. Let's assume box one is labeled oranges, box two is labeled apples, and box three is labeled apples and oranges. Now, we pick a fruit from box three. Box three *cannot* be oranges and apples because all are labelled incorrectly. If we pick an apple, Box three's label must be apple by elimination. Again, since all labels are incorrect, box two must be oranges and box one must be mixed."

"Excellent work. However, since no one solved it individually, I'm sorry to say one person will not receive ten points on the next test." Daniel looked around at the faces expecting to see sorrow from his decision. Instead he saw a glowing pride from each of his students. "Alternately, I've decided to give everyone ten points on the next test."

David Boiani

The class cheered and clapped.

"You've proven that teamwork and unselfishness can overcome any obstacle. Good work, young geniuses. That's all for today."

Daniel watches as his students filed out of the room, still buzzing about the free points toward the next test. He packed up his paperwork, placed his files into his case and exited the classroom. Up ahead were two students engaged in an animated conversation. As he advanced he recognized Julie and Michael. They stopped the conversation as he approached the couple.

"Hi Julie, Michael. Anything I can help you with?"

He looked over their faces and recognized fear on Julie's and anger on Michael's.

"No sir, we're just talking," Michael said.

Daniel smiled. "Julie, excuse us. I'd like a word with Michael in my classroom."

Julies eyes darted away as she turned to go.

"Wait, Julie..."

Daniel put his hand up to Michael's response. "Michael, let her go, for your own good. We need to talk."

Michael watched his girlfriend walk down the hall and leave the school.

"Follow me," Daniel said.

The pair entered the room, Daniel sat behind his desk and pulled up a chair for Michael. "Sit."

Michael did as he was told.

"Michael, have you ever heard of Reinhold Niebuhr?"

"No."

"He was a famous professor and theologian. He had some really fabulous quotes, one being 'All human sin seems so much worse in its consequences than its intentions'. Do you have an idea what that means?"

Michael shook his head.

"I don't believe you intend to hurt Julie. I think you care about her, partly from what she tells me about you and partly because I can see it on your face when you're with her. However, you need to stop being rough with her or I'll have to notify the authorities. That's the consequence of your actions. Whatever your intentions are, the end result will be you being arrested and losing the girl you care about. I don't believe that's what you want, nor do I believe you intend to hurt her. Are we in agreement so far?"

Michael looked away. "She does things sometimes that makes me feel...angry."

"What, exactly?"

"Talks to guys I don't know. Sometimes she goes places without telling me. I don't want to lose her."

"So, you want to build a prison to keep her in? You want to abuse her until she listens and follows every rule you impose on her? People are not possession's, Michael. A major part of truly loving someone is watching them in their freedom. Watching them achieve, interact, be successful in life, and earning respect for them."

Michael looked down and Daniel noticed a shameful look on his face.

"Michael, were you abandoned as a child? Ignored? Forgotten? Your actions toward Julie don't stem from anything she's done, they're your own insecurities and uncontrolled emotions, and the consequences of those insecurities and emotions will not be what you want them to be."

Daniel hung on that last sentence for a few moments to let the seriousness sink in. "Now, I can get you help. I have a friend who's a psychiatrist, Doctor Jason Phillips, he specializes in working with people who have insecurity issues and anger problems. I can set up something for you."

"I don't have any money."

"I'll take care of that, under one condition. You promise me you'll keep your hands off her. If you feel the rage build, the red mount, you walk away until you can calm yourself. If I witness anything to the contrary, the deal is off, and I go to the authorities."

Michael looked around uncomfortably as Daniel held his gaze into the young man's eyes.

"Michael, do we have a deal?"

"Okay."

Daniel reached out his hand and the boy took it. After they shook hands, Daniel said, "I'll be in touch with you with all of the pertinent information. You may go now."

As Michael made his way to the door Daniel called out, "Oh, and Michael." The boy turned. "I'll be watching you."

Michael nodded and left the room.


Daniel and Tim landed at the Manchester-Boston Regional Airport on Saturday morning. They took a taxi to Woodhaven resort, located on the bottom of the mountain, a short shuttle ride from Alpine Adventures. They pulled up to the resort, took their meager belongings and walked toward the front door. They both stopped in their tracks as they looked up at the scene in front of them. The mountain towered over the small resort with its snow-covered peaks in complete contrast with the early winter foliage of eastern white pine, eastern hemlock, balsam fir, and northern white-cedar. The contrast of colors created a natural rainbow form the range of greens of the pines to the pure white and silver shadows of the snowy mountain and finishing off with the most pure, electric, crisp, azure blue Daniel had ever seen. Daniel turned and smiled to Tim as they entered the front of the establishment.

"Hi, may I help you?" a cheery, attractive middle-aged woman said as they approached the front desk.

"Hello, we have a suite reserved through tomorrow," Tim said.

"Name, please."

"Tim Roberts."

"Yes, here we are, suite twenty-three." The attendant handed Tim a keycard, smiled and wished the pair and enjoyable stay. Ten minutes later, they were settled into their suite and ready to take on the mountain.

A few hours later they were in a shuttle on their way up the side of the mountain. He watched the snow-covered green pine foliage pass as a nervous anticipation took over his mind. He was nervous to experience such an extreme activity, yet excited to push the limits and boundaries of his comfort zone and reality. He glanced out of the window up into the vibrant blue sky just as a huge Bald eagle soared high above the trees. He watched as the elegance of the nation's emblem and mascot overtook him. He'd never actually seen a Bald eagle in person, the fierce beauty, and proud independence which symbolizes the strength and freedom of America overcame him and he felt a warm, heartfelt connection to the wild bird soaring majestically so high above him.

They reached the top of the ziplining course and were led one by one up a huge ladder leading to a platform situated in the top of the trees. Once locked into the structure by a clamp and line, Daniel looked out over the snow-capped side of the mountain and pine trees. He breathed in the freshest air his lunges had ever felt. This was one of those moments that would stay forever frozen in time in his mind and for once in his life he forgot he was a human, entrapped by society, a prisoner to his own expectations and responsibilities. For that one moment, he was as free and proud as the graceful eagle soaring alone through the crisp, clear New Hampshire sky.

The guide clamped the lead person, a young energetic male, onto the first zipline, reiterated the importance of a few rules and instructions, and the young man was off, soaring though the trees. The first line was short and relatively shallow and Daniel assumed it was to get the rider accustomed to the feel before riding the more extreme lines. There were only eight people in the group and soon Daniel was up. The instructor rambled off his rules and regulations and where to place his hands.

"Is this your first time ziplining?" the guide asked.

"Sure is."

"You picked quite a line for your maiden flight, my friend. Just relax and enjoy it. Are you ready?"

"Let's do this," Daniel responded.

"When you're ready, walk off the ledge."

Daniel did as he was instructed and suddenly was suspended above the snow-covered foliage, suspended in the middle of the trees, and gliding the short distance to the next platform. The feeling of flight was a new experience to him and surprisingly, he welcomed it without any sense of fear. He was hooked into the platform and he turned to watch Tim glide in next. When Tim was secured, he turned to Daniel.

"Well?"

"It's awesome."

Tim smiled. "It is."

The next line was high, long, and fast. Daniel watched the others soar through the sky and suddenly it was his turn. He jumped off the platform and instantly felt the wind on his face as he picked up speed and elevated quickly. He looked out in all directions, viewing the world from a new perspective, as a bird would. A feeling of freedom, immaculate spirit, and youth came over him. He landed on the next platform somehow different than before, pure and clean, without any negative thoughts or polluted feelings.

They walked a narrow, suspended bridge among the trees to the next platform where another line awaited them, this one longer and faster than the last.

They climbed ladders, traversed suspended bridges, and soared through the air like that Bald eagle Daniel witnessed on the way up, all while re-connecting with their youth and pure spirit. When the last line was completed, Daniel turned to Tim and said, "Thank you." Tim just smiled and nodded his head.

# Chapter Nine

Daniel returned home late Sunday afternoon. Madison met him as he entered.

"Hi, how was it?" she asked while moving in for a hug.

"Madison, it was amazing. We did the course twice, once each day. It's quite an experience. I want to take you and the kids sometime."

"Sounds great, but it'll be hard to fit us in with your schedule with Tim."

Daniel sensed the sarcasm. He held her body tight to his.

"I'm sorry, babe. Do you want me to stop?"

"No, of course not. I see how positively it is affecting you. I just feel...left out."

"I swear I'll make it up to you. We'll have adventures beyond your wildest dreams."

"Okay, the children missed you."

"Where are they?"

"Watching a movie. They don't know you're home yet."

Daniel kissed his wife and headed into the den and snuck up behind the couch where his son and daughter sat, eyes trained on the television.

"What's the movie about?"

"Daddy!" his son howled and jumped over the couch into Daniel's arms.

"Hi Dad," Emily added.

"Hi, you two. How are you both?"

"Dad, was it fun?" Logan asked.

"It was awesome. I'm going to take you guys soon."

"When, Dad?" Emily asked.

Daniel looked at his daughter, sat beside her and took her in his arms. "Soon, baby girl. I know I haven't been around as much lately, but I'll make it up to you guys and Mom." He kissed her on the top of her head.

"Okay, can I pick where we go first?"

Daniel smiled. "Sure, you can."

That night he made love to Madison three times with a revived energy and passion. They lay in bed exhausted, content, and happy. Madison placed her head on Daniel's chest.

"Wow, that was amazing. The best ever," she said.

"It was. I missed you."

"My body is still quivering. Did I complain about your excursions? I take it back. Go as much as you want."

Daniel laughed as they drifted off to sleep, their bodies bound together as one.


"Thomas Hobbes was a sixteenth century English philosopher who is considered one of the founders of modern political philosophy. He professed humans as being self-interested, egocentric beings, who are never happy with any amount of power or wealth who'd do anything to satisfy their own desires. Does anyone agree or disagree with Mr. Hobbes assessment of human nature?"

A few hands were raised, and Daniel called on a young man in the back row named Peter.

"Isn't it our instinct to be selfish, in a matter of our own survival?"

"That was Hobbes' belief. However, there are times when an altruistic state takes over. People giving to others without expecting or wanting anything in return. How do we factor that into the equation and still accept Hobbes' theory?"

Brain raised his hand to a few chuckles from his classmates.

"Yes, Brian?"

"If you know any of these altruists, I'd be happy to step in and be the object of their desires."

The classroom erupted in laughter and Daniel put his hand to his forehead to add to the humor.

"In all seriousness, people, let's take a deeper look into these altruists. Or, to be more precise, anyone who's ever given up their happiness for another."

Another hand shot up, this time from Tina, an attractive young woman in her first year of college.

"Yes, Tina?"

"How altruistic are most of these altruistic givers, anyway? I mean, most are so well off there isn't any danger of them parting with their well-being. I'd be much more impressed with a poor person giving to someone in need. They're really at risk but choose to do so anyway."

"Excellent deduction, Tina. Are these altruists seriously just trying to help people or are they doing it for a feeling it gives them; a way to feel better about themselves, hence, making themselves happier, which is actually a selfish priority?"

Daniel paced the room, pausing between sentences to assure that he had the room's full attention. "Now, let's discuss a serious topic which affects over half the families in the United States. Divorce. Do you think couples with children who divorce are selfish?"

Most of the class nodded in agreement.

"So, you think staying in a loveless marriage is an altruistic notion?" Daniel looked around as most of his students continued nodding.

"Does anyone disagree with this?"

Susan raised her hand.

"Yes, Susan?"

"I think it can be more complicated than that. I mean, if you stay in a marriage because of the love you feel for your children, isn't that self-serving as well? Wouldn't that be to protect your own feelings?"

"Not often, but sometimes I get to feel the excitement of a student who has worked out a lesson on his or her own and I feel ecstatic. This is one of those times. Very good, Susan. If every decision we make is ultimately tied to our own feelings, our own survival, our own well-being, then maybe Hobbes was right. Maybe we are selfish. I teach to help you students understand the world and its inhabitants. However, I also teach to feel that high when I know students have learned from my lesson. That is my self-serving desire which is why I teach."

"Mr. B, if you want to get high, surely some cannabis would be much easier and quicker," Brian said to a wave of laughter.

"On that note, we will end this lecture. Have a great day, my students and be safe."

As his students filed out of the classroom, Daniel checked his cell for messages. He received a voice mail from his psychiatrist friend, William Spencer.

*Hi, Daniel. I've met with Michael Simmons. I believe I can help him. He's built up rage and insecurities form his past which I feel can be rehabilitated. I'll see him twice a week and monitor his progress. Talk soon.*

Daniel put his phone in his pocket and headed home with a warm, gleeful feeling that had stemmed from an altruistic gesture.

# Chapter Ten

T he holidays fast approached as mid-December arrived and Daniel brooded over what to get Madison. He ruled out some kind of jewelry, as he'd bought her so many pieces through the years. He wanted this year to be special. He had decided to stop at the mall one afternoon for some ideas. As he checked his cell phone for missed calls or texts before starting the car, he noticed an email advert:

### *Aruba Caribbean Resort and Casino!*

*Come experience our Aruba get away for an all-inclusive weekend. We offer swimming, fine dining, gambling, and a beautiful beach front spa. Located along the Island's Palm Beach Strip, every room features its own private patio or balcony with a garden and/or ocean view. Click here to take advantage of this special, limited time offer!*

He followed the link and took down all the information needed then called the number setting up a trip for the third weekend in January. He received a printable pamphlet through email to be used as a physical gift. It contained pictures of the resort, available activities, and the dates they would be in attendance. Later that evening, he printed it, placed it in a small box, wrapped it, and hid it inside his dresser drawer. They were purchasing a Christmas tree that weekend and he would place it under the decorated tree then. He couldn't wait to see Madison's reaction to unwrapping it on Christmas day.

"Confucius was a Chinese philosopher, teacher, and political figure, born in 551 B.C. His teachings focused on creating ethical models of family and public interaction and setting educational standards. His basis was ethics and love. He taught people to treat others as they would themselves and he inspired his people with his positive outlook and warm, morally virtuous beliefs. Has anyone heard of the quote, 'It does not matter how slowly you go, as long as you do not stop.?'"

A few students raised their hands.

"How about, 'The will to win, the desire to succeed, the urge to reach your full potential—these are the keys that will unlock the door to personal excellence.'"

A dozen more hands went up.

"These are the types of inspiration proverbs Confucius passed on to his people, leading them into the age of Confucianism, and a better way of life. He was as important to his people as anyone throughout history."

# Chapter Eleven

The moment Daniel and Tim had returned from New Hampshire Daniel had started brainstorming about their next adventure. He remembered reading somewhere that bull-riding was the mightiest adrenaline rush in the world. He thought it was time to amp up the intensity of their exploits, but was amateur bull riding too much? Too dangerous?

*No. This is why we've agreed to this, to push the boundaries, the limits, and encounter the wildest, most extreme adventures the world has to offer.* He searched amateur bull riding and a few links appeared, all located in Texas. He clicked the first:

## ***Experience the thrill of riding a 1500 pound pissed off animal as you hold on for dear life!***

*If this entices you in any way, book a reservation and experience the thrill of a lifetime! Come visit our ranch in Rockdale, Texas. Discounts and group rates are available, and first-timers don't fret, we'll train you before you get anywhere near the beast.*

Daniel saved the website to his favorites. Without him even realizing it, the decision was made in the back of his mind the moment he read the heading. By the end of the evening he had all the pertinent information and booked the first weekend in January.

"Nice shot."

Daniel watched as Tim ran off four balls in a row, leaving only his three ball and the eight.

"Another round?" he asked his friend.

"Sure," Tim responded, as he lines up a cross corner shot on the three. It rattled in the pocket and popped back out a few inches from the hole.

Daniel returned with the drinks and handed a beer to Tim.

"I know what we're doing next."

"Already? Well, fill me in. You know suspense kills me."

"Bull-riding, in the heart of Texas."

Tim nearly spit his mouthful of Allagash Black Stout onto the table.

"Seriously? Are you trying to kill us?"

Daniel chuckled. "I thought you were the brave one, other than ghosts, that is."

"I also enjoy living, and ghost do freak me out but only because they're dead already."

"Well, bulls are alive. It's time to crank this up, push the boundaries a bit." Daniel sank two balls but missed a long cut on one of his two remaining.

Tim sank his three and left himself a cross side shot on the eight to win. "You know what, partner. If you're up for it…" He smiled as he stroked a perfect shot sending the eight into the side packet. "So am I."

Daniel spent the following weekend with his family. They purchased a Christmas tree, decorated it and the house, and spent the evening drinking eggnog, eating popcorn, and watching movies. The time spent away from them made him yearn to be with them more than ever before, and he respected the moments they created together. He placed Madison's gift under the tree and noticed her pick it up and examine it before they retired to their bedroom for the night.

"You'll never guess what it is," he said as they climbed into bed.

"If I guess correctly, will you tell me?"

"Of course."

"Is it…keys to a new car?"

"No."

"A puppy?" she said as she placed her head on his chest.

He turned to look at her.

"Another child?"

"My dear, I have no disillusion that I have any control over that."

She slapped his arm.

"You know I'd discuss it with you first before taking any action toward adding to this family. I'm content with the two beautiful children we've been blessed with already. You get one more guess."

She glanced at him and placed her head back down on his chest. "A trip for just you and me."

Daniel sat up with shock and wonder evident on his face. "Hey, how did you…?"

"I know you, Daniel. It wasn't hard to decipher that you feel guilty about your excursions with Tim. You wanted to make it up to me."

Daniel relaxed and pulled her body close to his as he brooded for a while. Finally, he responded, "Fine, but I'm not telling you the destination."

"Suit yourself, handsome. But I bet it'll be wonderful."

"Yes, it will be," he said.

They both fell into a deep sleep together.


"Socrates was credited as one of the founding fathers of Western philosophy. And the first moral philosopher of the Western ethical tradition of thought. Now, I know what you're thinking, my intellectual champions of grey matter; just what the heck is the Western ethical tradition of thought?"

"Glad you said it Mr. B, cause I had no freaking idea," Brian said.

Daniel smiled before continuing. "I'll outline the Western ethical tradition of thought for the sake of the classroom." He waked over to the chalkboard and wrote:


## The Five Core Ethical Streams in Western Philosophic Thought:

1. Virtue Ethics/Relational ethic

2. Deontology

3. Rights

4. Utilitarianism

5. Communitarianism


"Okay, now that we have that bureaucratic bullshit out of the way, let me explain it to you in terms that you can understand."

The classroom erupted in laughter.

"Go Mr. B!" someone yelled from the back of the room.

"The primary question of ethics brought forth in Western philosophical thought was, 'How shall I live'. Socrates based his beliefs and teachings on two concrete, never changing theories: One, knowledge is the key, and two, knowledges helps us to live the good life correctly. Socrates is famous for his method of incessant questioning which, has come to be known as the Socratic method. It's in this method that most of the early Platonic dialogues are conducted. He pointed out that human choice was motivated by the desire for happiness. Ultimate wisdom comes from knowing oneself. The more a person knows, the greater his or her ability to reason and make choices that'll bring true happiness.

"Socrates presents certain ethical standards. One of these standards is that the soul and the preservation of a pure soul is the most important thing. He goes on to explain that living well, living a fine life, and living justly are the same. This position illustrates another important aspect of Socratic ethics...Socrates believes that no one knowingly commits wrong. To commit wrong prevents achieving eudaimonia, thus no one would knowingly do so. In this view Socrates' ethics can be seen as the seeking of knowledge in order to live correctly and to live the happiest life. His insistent emphasis on the greater importance of the mind threatened Greek conventional wisdom, and he was sentenced to death by drinking a mixture of poison hemlock. So much for intelligent thought."

Another round of laughter took over the room.

"But, my wonderfully intellectually gifted students, let's not disrespect the importance of Socrates and his elevated, original thoughts with humor. He may have been the most important of all the philosophers from any generation. We can even see his teachings reflect upon the holiday season that's now upon us. Is it better to give than receive? Socrates would've argued the feeling of giving far exceeds the material items gained by receiving."

Brian piped up with, "I believe Socrates to be right, so, to help his cause. I'll accept any and all gifts from my classmates, just to make them feel better about themselves." This brough another round of laughter from the class.

"Brain, what an altruistic gesture. I'm sure Socrates would've been proud. This being our last class before the holiday break, I'd like to say enjoy yourselves and your families and above all, be safe."

Daniel watched as his students filed out one by one, each wishing him happy holidays and new year.

The Holidays rolled in and suddenly it was Christmas Eve. Daniel and Madison put the children to bed and placed all the presents under the tree, hung the stockings, and had a glass of wine together before deciding it was time to go to bed.

"I'll be up in a minute, beautiful."

Madison gave him a soft smile and headed up the stairs. Daniel studied the tree while taking inventory of his life and another year gone. They decorated the tree in red and white which gave it a stately, classy look. Madison had always relented to the two-color scheme and thought a variety of colors was more enjoyable for the children, but Daniel liked the simpler, nobler look. The holidays always put him in a somber mood as they represented time slowly evaporating before our eyes. This year he had a different mindset. He felt rejuvenated and connected to his past and his youth. Instead of feeling like he was slowly falling down a hill toward certain death, he felt like he was heading toward exciting new territory, with many new experiences yet to come. He'd even lost the extra weight he'd been carrying for the last decade. He had more energy and new attitude toward life in general.

He headed upstairs to join Madison in bed but turned into the master bathroom to brush his teeth. He looked in the mirror and noticed something...different. The lines around his eyes seemed softer, less visible. He crawled into bed next to Madison, who was already in a deep sleep. Shortly after, he joined her in slumber.

Daniel glanced out the window early Christmas day. Jack Frost had paid a visit, bringing frigid temperatures and a storm which changed the world into a moonscape of white. The children woke early, as equally excited about the changing landscape outside as they were about the numerous gifts under the tree. Daniel started a fire and the recognizable assortment of Christmas scents filled the air. The rainbow-orange crackling of the fire brought a thick, zesty, earthy scent which created a perfect combination with the fresh, clean, sharp scent of the Christmas tree. Daniel brewed a pot of coffee which added to the ensemble of pleasing aromas. *This is as Christmas should smell* he thought as he poured Madison and himself each a cup, then returned to sit by the tree to watch everyone open their gifts. The tree glittered and Daniel was amazed at how perfect it looked.

*If only our lives followed suit. If only we could feel this way all year* he thought.

After they opened their gifts, Daniel lead the children outside to break in one of their presents from Santa: a pair of sleds for the snow. The trio stepped outside as the wind blew the freshly falling snow around. Daniel stopped for a moment to experience the feeling to the fullest. There was a sharp, crispness in the air and Daniel immediately connected to his childhood. A strong gust whipped up and waltzed dreams through the air, the flakes dancing in a frenzied, hysterical pattern. He opened his mouth, catching a few rogue flakes on his tongue and smiled as the frozen goodness melted in his mouth. They headed for a hill a mile down the street as they ran, played, and threw snowballs at each other, laughing the whole time. Daniel could have been eight again, enjoying a virgin storm for the first time in any of those winters, so long ago.

Following a lengthy session of sledding, they returned home to a greeting of delicious scents coming from the kitchen as Madison prepared Christmas dinner. Daniel set the table for eight as both sets of parents were coming to celebrate the holiday. With the table set,

Daniel settled in on the couch next to his children. The Grinch played on the television.

"Daddy, why does the Grinch want to ruin Christmas for the Whos?" asked Logan.

"He isn't a very happy individual, so he wants everyone else to feel that way."

"Why?" Emily asked.

"When people are unhappy they want others to experience the same, so they have company."

"But why does he change his mind at the end?"

"Well, when he finally realizes his misery won't affect the people of Whoville, his heart grows, and he decides to join them in being happy and spreading love instead of hate."

The doorbell rang sending his children in a frenzy to greet their grandparents. Daniel remained on the couch a moment longer and watched as the Grinch brought all the presents back to Whoville.

*If only life was so simple, spread love instead of hate,* he thought before rising and heading for the ruckus at the front door.

Minutes later, dinner was served and the whole family feasted on a traditional Christmas dinner: turkey, stuffing, cranberry sauce, sweet potato casserole, and all the side dishes and trimmings. After dinner, everyone gathered around to exchange and open gifts with the grandparents. Madison served pumpkin and pecan pie for dessert. Daniel gave his wife a look as his children opened new cell phones from Madison's parents. Daniel understood the importance of technology and how it has changed society, however, he could never warm up to six and eight year-old children having their own phones. He was old-fashioned in ways and he knew It would be an adjustment he would have to accept.

When all the holiday festivities were concluded, their guests departed and Logan and Emily were tucked into their beds having already fallen asleep, Daniel brought his gift to Madison for her to open by the Christmas tree.

"Thank you, love," she said, as she started unwrapping the gift. Daniel watched as her excitement grew by the moment. Finally, the little box was free from its covering. Madison pulled the top off and picked up the brochure describing the resort and its offerings.

"Aruba! Oh Daniel, thank you!"

"It's just a long weekend, my love. We leave Friday afternoon and arrive home Monday night. We can go the third weekend of January, if that works for you."

"Oh, Daniel. I love it!" she said as she jumped into his arms. Shortly after, they made love on the floor in front of the Christmas tree under the cover of a soft warm blanket. In the bliss of post lovemaking, he watched her fall asleep, a slight smile on her pink lips. She was beautiful, and the happy, youthful look on her face reminded him of the day he met her...

*Daniel walks to the bar to order another scotch. The wedding of Jason, his good friend from college, was an enchanting evening so far. However, nothing could prepare him for what was about to happen. A beautiful woman approaches and smiles slightly as she steps up next to him and orders a glass of wine. She turns to look at him directly and Daniel notices every detail. The shape of her face, her deep, intoxicating eyes, the subtle yet exotic curve of her hip as she settles into the seat next to him.*

*"Hi, I'm Daniel, a good friend of the groom," he says and extends his open hand in her direction. He notices the slight pause as she contemplates his greeting before accepting his hand in hers. He feels an electric current run through them and notices a flash in her eyes as she feels the same. A few strands of hair fall from her bangs into her eyes and she quickly, sexily, pushes them aside.*

*"Hi, Daniel, I'm Madison, Abigail's cousin."*

*Daniel is enraptured with everything about Madison. He notices her subtle sexiness, her admirable classiness, her quick wit and sharp sense of humor. She instantly makes him feel alive, like he was just born and every secret of the universe lies behind those dazzling eyes.*

*They spend the remainder of the evening together and plan a date together for the following weekend. On the ride home, Daniel's mind is consumed with thoughts of her. He'd been with three women in his life but somehow the encounter Madison was unlike anything he had experienced before. There was something deeper; a connection that exceeded the usual simple physical attraction. He arrives home and collapses on his bed while still donning his tux. His eyes close and he drifts off with Madison filling his mind and heart.*

Daniel studied Madison's face as she slept. A few lines have started to become clearer around her eyes and wrinkles have started to show around her neck, however she was still the most beautiful woman Daniel had ever seen. Their experiences together had strengthened their bond, and he couldn't imagine falling asleep next to anyone else.

He watched her chest rise and fall in rhythm, her breathing was slow and peaceful. He kissed her forehead, wrapped his arm around her, closed his eyes, and joined her in the world where anything is possible.

# Chapter Twelve

hristmas break flew by and suddenly it was New Year's Eve. Daniel set up a dinner date with long-time friend from college John Sullivan, who took Daniel and Tim under his wing their first year. He was a senior and five years their elder. He showed them around campus, introduced them to his friends, and invited them to many weekend excursions. Being older and having started a family at a young age, John's children were now in college. Daniel and he had kept in touch throughout the years and made it a point to get together at least once a year as they still lived relatively close to each other. They pulled into John's long driveway and approached the stately, prestigious house. Daniel rang the bell and turned to smile at Madison. The door flew open.

"Daniel, so glad to see you! Maddie, you look as beautiful as ever."

"Thank you, John," Madison replied.

Daniel embraced his friend and said, "John, how've you been? Where's Jennifer?"

"She's in the kitchen cooking you two up a wonderful dinner. Follow me."

John led them through the foyer, the dinning room, and into the kitchen where Jennifer appeared, apron and all.

"Daniel, Madison! So good to see you!"

Daniel gave her a robust hug. "Like wise, Jenny. How've you been?"

"We're doing very well, thank you."

Madison followed up with a hug of her own and the two ladies poured glasses of wine for everyone and Madison asked if she could help in the kitchen. Daniel and John moved to the den, wine in hand.

"So, my friend...what's new, how are the kids?" John asked as he sat on the couch.

"Happy and healthy. They're both good students and seem to be hard-working."

"That's wonderful. You're lucky, my friend."

Daniel pondered where he'd take the discussion as he glanced at his long-time acquaintance. He noticed John had added a few pounds around the mid-section, his temples had greyed a bit more and the lines around his eyes had become more prominent. It had been a year since their last visit and John's age had started to show. The wives entered the room with a freshly opened bottle of red.

"How are Peter and Crystal?" Daniel asked. He noticed a flinch before John answered his query.

"They're well, both away. Peter is still at Syracuse and Crystal is in her first year at NYU."

"That's great. Do you miss them? Now that they're both out of the house, I mean. It must be an adjustment."

Daniel noticed a shadow play over John's face. A slight frown appeared as he peered into his wine glass and reached for the bottle for a refill. The ladies felt the heaviness of the moment and their conversation ceased, as their attention turned fully to John's reply. He took a long sip of the restored liquid and met Daniel's eyes.

"Have you even heard the song 'Cats in the Cradle' by Harry Chapin? Of course you have, everyone has. Well, I never truly understood it, I mean, yeah, I get it, he misses his son, but I never fully understood the depth and meaning of those lyrics until I lived through it. When they were young, I was so busy, you know, building my life, my business, and doing everything to hold together the seams of my life, of our life..." He pulled Jennifer in close to him. "I always thought there'd be more time to spend with them, to connect and create memories they'd never forget, but honestly there weren't enough of those memories. There could never be enough. Even today when I look at them, I see them both as children with a sparkle in their eyes and that pure, innocent look on their faces. What I wouldn't give now to go back and see those faces again, to spend more time with them, back when they idolized us as their parents and all they wanted was our attention. Then one day, you wake up and realize they've changed. They've moved on to their friends, their peers and hanging with old dad isn't cool anymore." Daniel noticed a tear fall from Jennifer's eye as she kissed John on the forehead. "Well, you feel this pain inside. Not a sharp pain, but a dull ache that's always there just below the surface eating away at your heart and your sanity. Maybe it's just that you miss them. Maybe it's a reminder of our mortality as time goes by and seasons change, the calendar flips, and they grow older before our eyes. When I hear that song, it brings me to tears every time." John turned to look Daniel in the eyes and Daniel noticed his eyes were wet. "Of all the advice I've ever given you, please take this and follow it, my friend. Spend every moment you can with them. Love them and prove to them they come first, no matter what. Create memories—not only for them, but for you. You'll have the rest of your life to be alone together, but the time with them is limited because, just as the song states, 'He'd grown up just like me, my boy was just like me.' The memories I do have help cure that dull ache, but it never goes away."

Daniel rose, approached his friends and kissed Jenny on the cheek while patting John on the shoulder. "I hear you loud and clear and will remember your words of wisdom. Thank you."

The mood lightened up and the two couples had a delicious dinner, their fill of wine, played a few card games and topped the night off with champagne and a dance as the ball dropped in Times Square and the music played. Shortly after midnight, they wished their friends a happy, healthy and prosperous new year before heading home. Minutes later, they arrived home and Daniel went straight upstairs as Madison paid the babysitter and saw her out. He woke each of his children, told them he loved them, wished them a happy new year, and kissed them goodnight. He vowed from this moment forward to dedicate himself as their father and create as many memories as possible.


Daniel and Tim landed in Austin, Texas on Saturday morning and checked into their hotel. They stopped for breakfast and then headed out on the one-hour drive to Rockdale for their scheduled training before the real deal that evening at 8:00 pm. They enjoyed the transformation of the Texas landscape as they moved away from the city vistas to the farms and ranches of Rockdale. They arrived at Rockdale Ranch and pulled up to the small building offset from an imposing barn.

"This is it, partner. We register, then head to that monster barn for training."

"Let's do this," Tim said, as he hopped out of the car and headed for the door. Daniel followed close behind.

"Hi, may I help you two...cowboys?" the young lady asked from behind the counter.

Daniel looked down at his attire before inspecting his friends. Fitted Jeans and polo shirts hugged their bodies with hiking boots on their feet.

"We have a reservation for riding lessons and an actual bull-ride tonight."

"Names, please?"

As Daniel gave their names and squared up everything at the desk, Tim wandered into a small shop offset from the office. Cowboy hats, cowboy boots, flannel shirts and cowboy cut Wrangler Jeans flooded the shop. Daniel joined him.

"We're live in the barn in thirty minutes."

"Let's grab some gear. To act like a cowboy, you must look the part."

Daniel laughed. "Sure."

"Can I help you boys?" the woman from behind the counter asked. Daniel noticed how naturally beautiful she was, now out in the open. Her perfectly proportioned figure flowed under her tight flannel shirt and jeans. He felt a twinge in his groin but quickly buried it. His natural male instincts had been dormant for years and he couldn't remember the last time he became erect from another woman other then his wife. He noticed a spark in Tim's eye as he turned to greet her. Daniel's body relaxed and he felt at ease.

"Yes, you can ma'am. We'd like to look like cowboys."

"Well, I can definitely help a couple Yankees like you," she said with a chuckle. Looking at her closely, Daniel guessed she was in her early thirties, easily ten years his junior.

After settling on the woman's choices, they changed and left the shop decked out in cowboy gear. Daniel walked out first followed by Tim with her phone number on a small piece of paper, which he proudly displayed to Daniel as they entered the barn for their lesson.

"Sierra? Damn, even her name is sexy," Daniel said as he read the small paper.

Tim winked and they stepped up to the front desk. A man turned to them as they approached and Daniel noticed he was a cowboy—a *real* cowboy—with a high-crowned, wide brim cowboy hat, high top cowboy boots with pointed toes, denim jeans hidden under a brown pair of leather chaps, and soft leather cowboy gloves. As Daniel took in the rest of the barn he was overwhelmed with the sights and sounds. It felt like he was being transformed into the wild, wild west, with cowboys, horses, and bulls as far as he could see, all organized in multiple rings filled with dirt, enclosed in six-foot fencing. The air was heavy with dust being kicked up by the activities happening around them. Daniel choked up ma bit as he spoke, the dust getting the better of his throat.

"Hi, we're here for a bull-riding lesson. Daniel Burton."

The cowboy spit a lob of brown spit obviously discolored by the wad of tobacco in his cheek. He had a goatee which resembled Buffalo Bill's famous facial hair.

"Ever ride before?"

"No," Daniel answered. "Nope," Tim followed.

"What a surprise. Yaw'll be instructed on the basics, most importantly, how to be safe and keep yourself alive. Pissed off bulls don't have symphony for city folk. Matter of fact, they seem to seek them out." Another wad of brown saliva hit the dirt. "Brody will be over to take it from here. Just do everything he says and yaw'll be fine."

"Brody? Seriously?" Tim said with a smirk. "I thought Brody was just a name used in westerns?"

Another wad of spit, this time moving ever so closer to Tim's foot and his newly purchased boots. "Both of you read and sign this waiver form."

They did as informed when suddenly, another cowboy appeared.

"Daniel? I'm Brody Carson, follow me."

They glanced one last time at the spitting cowboy and followed Brody into the center of the barn. They entered a ring which sported a mechanical bull in the center.

"You'll each be trained on Toro, then you'll get a test ride that you must pass to ride the real thing." Brody spoke with less of a western twang and Daniel guessed he wasn't brought up on a western ranch.

Tim turned to Brody. "So, this bull we're going to ride, is he big?"

Brody's gaze stayed onto Tim a few seconds too long before he answered. "As beginners, you'll be riding the most docile of our bulls. He weighs about one-thousand pounds, which is why what I teach you here is of the upmost importance. This isn't a game, gentlemen. You could both be seriously hurt."

"Hence the waivers..." Daniel cut in.

"Yes, the waivers sever us from any liability if we hold up our end of the bargain. There's always the possibility of an uncontrollable accident. Of course, we take every precaution to prevent that from occurring." Brody looked from Daniel to Tim and noticed the tense, nervousness as the discussed the dangers. Brody smiled, revealing a brilliant white set of teeth which Daniel thought to be an exception for a cowboy. He always assumed they all had tobacco stained, yellow teeth. "Don't worry, relax and have fun. You'll be fine as long as you listen to what I'll teach you."

He taught them how to properly mount the animal, how to wrap their riding hands in the bull rope and secure a solid grip. He taught them how to keep their weight on the inside of their thighs and to lean forward so their chest is over the bull's shoulders. "Now as you wait for the start, be calm and focus. Take a deep breath and relax. The animal can sense a jittery rider and he'll taste victory. You need to show him you're the boss and don't fear him. An experienced rider will tell you this is the most difficult part of the ride. The calm before the storm. Controlling that tension."

Daniel mounted the fake bull.

"We're going to start slow and tame at first and as you get the feel of it I'll quicken the pace and the intensity."

Daniel felt the metal, plastic, and rubber move underneath him. He glanced at Tim whose eyes were wide and fixed on his every move.

"Okay, good. Now as Toro bucks lean forward and squeeze your legs, keep a tight grip on the rope. Keep your hips centered and square. That's it, good Daniel. I'm going to quicken the pace now. Use your free arm as a counter-balance to your body. That's an important part of staying on the animal. Feel the buck, move with the buck, wave after wave. Good! Now I'm really going to kick it up a notch. If he throws you, immediately scramble to your feet and head for the nearest gate. Our cowboys will move in as soon as they realize you're dismounting. They're trained professionals and know how to keep you safe. Okay, brace yourself Here we go!"

Suddenly, the frequency and intensity of the bucks accelerated and before he knew what was happening, Daniel was flying through the air and landing on his backside. He quickly rose to his feet and jumped over the closest gate to the applause of his teacher and his friend.

"Well done! Now, obviously, a living, breathing animal is much more powerful and unpredictable, so you need to remember everything we talked about here and never lose your focus. Next..." Brody said as he looked at Tim. After Tim took his turn, they each took a few more runs at Toro and Brody deemed them ready to ride the real thing.

They spent the afternoon at a local music festival and had dinner at a steak house before heading back to the ranch for their scheduled rides.

"Nervous?" Daniel asked Tim who was enjoying the Texas landscape from the passenger seat.

"Nope. I fear ghosts, not animals."

"Not even a thousand pound pissed off bull?"

"Well, maybe a bit, but animals love me. I'm sure he and I will come to an understanding."

"Oh really? An understanding as to why you're sitting your ass on his back?"

"Sure, It's all about communication, like every other relationship."

"So now you know bull-speak? Good to know."

"I can communicate with my body language. He'll understand."

"Glad you're so confident. I'm shitting my pants, but it feels exhilarating. We're going to experience something amazing that most don't have the opportunity to experience."

"Hey, stop off at a convenience store for me. I need to pick something up."

Daniel glanced over at Tim. "Sure."

After the short pit stop, they pulled into the ranch lot and entered the barn.

"Look who's returned. I was taking bets on whether you two would show up or not," the tobacco spitting Buffalo Bill cowboy said before he let another glob of brown spit fly.

"Actually, I wouldn't have missed it for the world," Tim said, before firing his own brown wad of shit, which landed on the toe of the Cowboy's boot.

"If my bull wasn't going to kick the shit out of yaw'll in a few minutes, I would myself. Enjoy your ride," Buffalo Bill replied. Tim winked as Daniel pulled him away. Brody, having noticed the commotion, walked over to them.

"Welcome back. Don't mind Billy there, he's a bit morose toward tourists."

"Billy? No shit, his name is Billy?"

"Yes."

"How many cowboys use the word morose?" Tim asked. "You aren't a native Texan, are you?

Brody just smirked and led them to a vacated ring in the middle of the barn.

"Okay, in that stall across the ring is Bone Collector. You can climb onto the platform to see him before you ride him. It can help to see the animal and envision being on his back first."

"Bone...Collector? Are you serious?" Daniel asked.

"That was his name a long time ago. He's old now and much more pleasant then he was in his fighting days. We just use him for first-timers now."

"That's not comforting," Daniel said.

"I got this bitch. He'll be eating out of my hand," Tim said.

They followed Brody around the ring to the platform. They climbed the stairs and looked down at their opponent. He had the blackest coat Daniel had ever seen and in the glint of the light almost looked blue. Although being an elder bull, his muscles flexed and shimmered as he snorted, and his hoofs raked at the dirt under his body. Daniel reached over to give him a pat on the back. He noticed the horns protruding from the top of his head.

"His horns are huge. I, uh, thought they would've been filed down or something?"

"There are places that'll dehorn them, but we feel it's inhumane. Why castrate this beautiful animal? Their horns are prideful to them. You wouldn't want a bull-ride that was unfair, would you? Just remember what I taught you and you'll be fine. We're live in ten minutes, so decide who'll ride first."

Brody walked away, leaving them to ponder who goes first and their decision to attempt the feat in the first place.

"There's no backing out now. There's no way I'd give Buffalo Bill that satisfaction."

"Nope, we're doing this. I'll go first. It was my idea."

Daniel put on a vest, chaps and a required helmet for amateurs. Brody appeared with six cowboys who Daniel guessed were there to save his ass once he was thrown from the beast. He climbed the stairs onto the platform above Bone Collector, took one last look around the barn and at Tim, and readied himself to mount the beast. The next six seconds were a flash in his mind, but at the same time seemed to last forever. He felt a rush of adrenaline kick in and he lowered his body onto the bull. He felt the animal's muscles tense up, almost as if he knew the challenge was on, and he wasn't about to let some amateur Yankee beat him at his own game. Suddenly the gate opened, and he was engaged in a violent dance with one of the strongest animals on the planet. He felt himself slip but held on tight and fought to keep in sync with the bucking bull. As he regained his balance, it felt vaguely like he was floating just above the bulls back, bracing himself for the contact of every buck. He didn't see anything around him; the barn, Tim, Brody or the cowboys ready to save his life. It was just him and the bull connected in a primal dance, their souls connected as one as they continue their violent waltz. Suddenly, the beast bucked and sent Daniel forward with his weight shifting over the front instead of his feet. One last buck caught Daniel on the backside and sent him spiraling through the air, landing in a heap some ten feet form the animal. He scrambled to his feet and took the quickest route to the fence, leaping over it and landing safely on the other side. He jumped up and looked back into the ring just in time to see the cowboys had distracted Bone Collector just enough for him to make his exit. A euphoric feeling of adrenaline overcame him, and he instantly wanted to ride him again.

Brody ran over from the other side of the ring. "Daniel, that was excellent! You stayed on for five seconds."

"Five seconds? That's it? It felt like a minute, at least."

"You lose the perception of time on a ride. Your mind enters a zone you don't usually visit. You did an amazing job. Tim, they'll re-load The Collector and you can take your turn in fifteen."

Daniel put his hand on Tim's shoulder. "Good luck."

"I got this. Piece of cake."

Tim walked away toward the loading platform. The bull had calmed a bit and was grazing around the ring as the Cowboys gathered him and led him back into the loading chute. Tim stood above the animal, talking to the Collector as if he were a friend he happened to stumble upon. Daniel heard the snort of the bull and thought, *maybe he can speak to him.* Moments later, Tim lowered himself onto the wide back of the bull and the gate flew open.

The next few moments happened in a flash. The Collector jumped out of the chute, bucking like a champion. Tim, who was leaning too far forward, was instantly thrown off, landing on his ass twenty feet from the beast. Suddenly, the animal charged him, horns down, back up, and spittle flying from his snout. Tim froze as he looked up at the oncoming animal. Tim closed his eyes and covered his head with his arms and curled up in a fetal position. Two cowboys swiftly jumped in front of the fallen rider, causing the bull's charge to veer off to the side, just missing Tim's limp figure. As the animal turned back for another run at the irritating human, a third cowboy picked Tim up and led him to the side of the ring and over the fencing, landing in a heap on the outside. Daniel ran over to check on the status of his friend.

"Tim! You okay?"

Daniel saw terror on Tim's face as he sat up and turned to Daniel.

"Hell yeah. Lucky bastard caught me off guard."

"What happened to speaking to him?" Daniel replied with a chuckle. "You sure it was bull-speak you were using?"

"Funny. Help me the hell up."

Suddenly a huge wad of brown saliva landed on Tim's boot. They turned to see Buffalo Bill walking away back to his desk at the front of the barn. His shoulders were shaking from laughing so hard. He turned one last time to look at his fallen adversary and said, "City slickers, gotta love em…"

# Chapter Thirteen

A s she slipped out of her pants and into a satin white nightgown bordered in lace the curve of Madison's hip projected from her panties. He rose and pulled her to him as his hand reached up under her gown.

"Daniel, what's gotten into you? You want to do it again? It's been years since we made love three times in the same day."

"Are you complaining?"

"No, of course not, tiger. Just wondering what has gotten into you."

"It was amazing, Madison. Riding that bull felt like I was young and free...like I was fifteen again. I guess the sexual desire stems from that."

"Really? So, explain to me exactly how it felt."

Daniel released his embrace on his wife and sat up. "Imagine being totally focused to the point that you hear or see nothing else but the back and head of the bull. It's a fast, violent constant fight for position, ultimately turning into a fight for survival. It's primal, your soul fills with adrenaline—it's almost as if you're outside your body, looking down on yourself and the bull. It's simply amazing Madison. Want to give it a try sometime?"

"Um, no. I'll stick to next weekend and Aruba."

Daniel smiled and pulled her back to him and their bodies connected for a third time.

"Today, my genius students, I'm going to toss out my own academic lesson. I'd originally planned a lecture on Walter Benjamin, however, I feel like trying something different."

Daniel glanced around the room at the bright, attentive eyes all drawn on him.

"Does anybody object to that or would you rather open up your textbooks to page 158, Walter Benjamin: *Historicism and Historical Materialism*?"

The classroom erupted in a chorus of boos.

"Okay, then, we'll experiment a bit. I'm going to ask all of you a question. It will be a personal question which you don't have to answer. However, if you feel the need to engage in the discussion, it'll be an open forum. No hands, no rules, jump in and out as you wish and say what's on your mind. Understood?"

Daniel watched as all the students nodded.

"Great. The question: What are the highest and lowest points of your life, and why?"

The students looked around at one another, none wanting to be the first to speak.

"A bit of hesitation? Okay, I understand. I'll kick this off answering my own question."

Daniel paced the front of the room as he gathered his thoughts. He sat on the front of his desk and began.

"I could say the obvious. Getting married, having children, purchasing my first home, and all those experiences are, of course, some of the greatest experiences of my life. However, I'm at a different stage of life than all of you, so I want to put all of that aside and talk about something that you, my genius students, will have an easier time relating to." Daniel paused, more for effect than anything. He'd learned over the years a little drama and timing was all it took to give a lecture and keep the young minds of his students interested and intrigued. He took a deep breath and began.

"I remember a cold, rainy night many years ago. I was eight and I'd taken a ride to the grocery store with my mother. As we pulled into the lot to find the closest parking spot to the store, I noticed something on the far side of the lot which was dark and vacant. A puppy. Wet, cold, skinny, and alone, wandering around not knowing where he was going. I immediately informed my mother of the stray and she drove over to see if we could help. The lot was surrounded by main streets and highways, so the probability of this puppy making it through the night was slim. Closer now, I could see he was a golden retriever, which begs the question, why was a Golden Retriever puppy lost and alone in the middle of a grocery store parking lot? That mystery, my friends, was never solved. We parked and tried to coax the little guy close enough so we could grab him. My mother kept calling and he'd come within six feet or so, then would turn and run off. She looked at me and said, 'You try, Daniel. You have a way with animals.' On the first try the puppy crept up close enough to sniff my hand and I pet him on his little head. Shortly after, he was safe inside our car and on his way to his new home. I felt an enormous amount of relief knowing he was safe. To this day, I know we saved his life that night. He and I had a special connection. I was truly his human and he never felt as safe except when he was with me. He went on to live ten fulfilling years, but passed away the summer before my eighteenth birthday, which, by the way, happened to be my low point."

Sympathetic articulations filled the room as Daniel pushed himself off the desk and paced the room once again. "Does anyone want to share their thoughts?" Daniel searched the young faces in the room looking for a willing expression. John, a usually quiet individual and academically average student, raised his hand.

"John, go ahead."

"The low point of my life was moving away from my girlfriend in my junior year I high school. We moved from the west coast, Fresno California, just east of Monterey, to New York. She was my fist love and I didn't speak to my parents for a month after we moved."

"I'm sorry, John. That's a terrible experience to go through as a young person. Sometimes life pushes and pulls us in different directions that, at the time, feel tragic. Healing from these life changes as adolescence and overcoming them is part of maturing into an adult. What was your high point?"

"Being able to study at Princeton University. I was a good student, but not superb. My parents both come from middle class, blue-collar families. I'm still not sure how they pulled off getting me into this school, but I'm forever grateful. This is my chance to change my life-course. Break the chain of blue-collar laborers that my family has been destined to follow."

"I'm glad you notice and respect the opportunity given to you by your parents and this school. The key is to remember that every time you seem overwhelmed by the work and the studies, remember how lucky you are to be here. Thank you for your story, John. Does anyone else want to share their thoughts with the class?"

Daniel searched the room for eager eyes, and he noticed Kim in the back row slowly raise her hand.

"Kim, go ahead."

"My low point was the passing of my grandmother, Eleanor. She was my best friend. We did everything together. Shop, watch television, dine out...she taught me how to play cribbage and we kept an ongoing count of our wins and losses on a small pad. We played the night before she passed from a heart attack last year. I miss her not just in the way someone would normally miss their grandmother, but also as if I lost my best friend as well. I keep the small pad in my nightstand drawer and take it out every night. 138-92. That was the score when she passed. She was in the lead. She was the best cribbage player around."

Kim put her head down and fought back tears and she attempted to regain her composure.

"My high point was reading a letter she'd written me in preparation of her death. She told me how much I meant to her and how proud of me she was. She said not to fret or cause a fuss over her because shell be in a happy place, waiting for all of us to join her someday. It doesn't kill the pain, but it does dull it a bit when I think of her in Heaven, playing cribbage and waiting for me to join her so we can continue our game."

Daniel walked back to Kim and put his hand on her shoulder.

"Thanks for sharing. I'm so glad you were able to find some comfort in her letter. She was a smart woman to prepare that for you."

Daniel walked to the front of the room and before he could speak again, Brian spoke suddenly without any indication it was coming.

"My father used to beat my mother and us when we were young. Being the oldest, ten years old at the time, I stood up to him one night as he towered over my mother after having struck her and bringing her to the floor again. I got up in his face and told him to get out or I'll call the cops. He looked at me for a moment that seemed like an eternity with his dark eyes boring into mine. I'll never know exactly what I saw in the next few seconds. At first it was pure anger and hatred, but then I saw a change. Was it pride? Pride that his eldest boy was finally becoming a man? Respect that I had the guts to stand up to a man twice my size? When I first spoke and put my chest up to his, I was ready for him to strike me. I braced myself, but it never came. After the look in his eyes changed, he turned and walked out, never to return. That was the best moment of my life. Ironically, it was also the worst."


Daniel stepped outside to settle his emotions and get some air before his next lecture. Never in his teaching career had he remembered being so affected by a classroom discussion than he was moments ago. Brian's ability to open up and make himself vulnerable to the class was a benchmark in his teaching. He was reaching his students. He was making a difference not only in their education, but in their lives.

He sat on a bench and breathed in the crisp, cold, pure January air. His eyes settled on small plastic bag blowing around in the gusty winter wind. He watched in for a few minutes and thought the flight of the bag resembled life; we're all floating around under the illusion we control our lives and destinies, however, the reality is we may control much less than we realize. Get on the wrong flight on the wrong day and it may be your last. Notice a lump one morning and you may be in battle for your life. Cancer has no omissions. It accepts everyone it can onto its list without apparent rhyme or reason. The vague, randomness of life is enough to emotionally paralyze anyone.

The bag flipped over in the breeze and was lifted into the canopy of an old oak tree where it became stuck on the end of a branch. It fluttered as the cold air pushed and pulled against it. Daniel rose to go back inside and teach his next class. He walked up to the door, opened it, paused, and turned to get one last image of the lonely bag. Suddenly, a gust came and lifted it out of the tree, high into the sky. The bag had prevailed and found is freedom. Daniel walked inside, rejuvenated and refreshed, welcoming the challenge of the rest of his life.

* * *

Waiting patiently for Madison to shower and dress, Daniel looked out across the Caribbean Sea, captivated by the breathtaking beauty. The water was so blue it was hard to tell where it stopped and the sky started, the only clue being the few wispy, white clouds high in the Aruba sky giving away the skies camouflage. He and Madison had never been to Aruba, and their first hour's experience left nothing to be desired. The resort was simply enthralling. Their hotel was built right on the beach with pure white sand surrounding them in every direction, creating a tropical beachfront oasis. Strategically placed throughout the encompassing sand were countless pools, tiki bars, private huts, and cabanas. It was exactly what Daniel envisioned from the ad, an island get-away where you can enjoy your privacy but also have the amenities that top-quality resorts offer, top-of-the-line restaurants, entertainment, and gambling. Daniel turned as he heard the bathroom door open followed by his wife entering the room in a classy little black dress. The image immediately took him back to their wedding day...

*Daniel glances patiently at the door awaiting his bride. He feels his blood pumping excitingly through his veins as his anticipation reaches a frenzied state as the door opens slowly and an angel in white comes into focus. As Madison approaches, their eyes meet, and Daniel feels every step she takes as if it were his body walking down the aisle. Their eyes lock, and Daniel melts inside. His heart overflowing from the happiness he feels as she steps up and stops by his side. He smiles and almost drops his head to kiss her. She reads his bodies reaction to her and her eyes grow large, bringing him out of his daze. He straightens up and smirks. They both chuckle lightly and turn to the priest. He can only breathe in and hope—*

"Well, are you just going to sit there and stare at me all day without speaking? How do I look?"

Daniel is snapped back to the reality of the present day.

"Wow, you look amazing. You brought back the memory of our wedding day."

A smile overtook Madison's face. "Thank you," she replies as she did a pirouette, revealing every angle of her body.

"Maybe we should skip dinner and just go to bed," Daniel said as he embraced her, holding her body tightly to his.

"Not a chance, buster. I've been waiting for this dinner all week."

Daniel smiled, released his wife, and led her to the door, holding it open as she walked by into the luxurious hallway.

Minutes later, they were seated in a secluded corner overlooking the sea in one of the top Caribbean restaurants in the world. Madison ordered tequila-lime shrimp, and Daniel followed with *Martinique*, a griller snapper with creole sauce. Madison took a sip of her Chi Chi and asked, "So, was riding a bull everything you thought it would be?"

"More, it was an amazing experience. You should try it. I'll take you sometime."

"I think I'll pass. Riding on the back of an angry two-thousand-pound animal is not my idea of a good time."

Daniel laughed. "It's not as bad as it seems. You become one with the bull. The key is not to fight the beast but move with him in some kind of primal dance."

"So, what went wrong with Tim?"

"He fought the bull and got thrown within two seconds."

"Well, that would probably be me. As I said, I'll pass."

After dinner, the couple had another round of drinks before returning to their room. They made love as a warm Caribbean breeze blew through the open windows and the brilliant moon shone down and reflected off the calm, yet massive sea.


Daniel woke in the middle of the night and couldn't get back to sleep. He threw on some casual clothes and headed to the casino, a five-minute walk from their room. He stopped at the ATM to grab some cash for a couple hands of blackjack. When the screen appeared to enter the amount of the withdrawal, he typed in $100, but then hesitated.

*I wonder what it feels like to let it all ride on one hand? I need to experience that.*

He re-entered the amount, pressed confirm transaction and the $20 bills cascaded out below. He picked them up and headed for an open table. He spotted one with a young woman dealing at an unlimited bet table. Something about her caught his eye. It wasn't sexual attraction, it was something about her innocence. She looked like the girl next door and he found he was attracted to her pure, honest look. Sometimes decisions are based on instinctual reactions that cannot be explained, and Daniel's instinct told him this was the dealer for him. The table had two other players, an old woman with a large pile of chips in front of her and a middle-aged man who seemed to be at the end of his rope. His hair was a mess from running his hands through it and his shirt was wrinkled. Daniel wondered just how long he'd been playing and how much he'd already lost. The man took the last sip of his beer and pushed one remaining chip in front of him. Daniel sat at the end of the table, a warm smile came over his lips as he pushed the bills forward. "Hi," he said.

"Hello," she said as she counted the money. "Buy in, two thousand, five-hundred."

The pit boss came over and monitored the transaction. "All good," he said, and the dealer scooped up the money and pushed the correct amount of chips in front of Daniel.

"This place is beautiful, you must enjoy living here," Daniel said as he pushed the complete stack of chips in front of him.

She smiled and replied, "I love it. There are worse destinies in life than waking up in paradise every morning. Good luck, sir."

Noticing the large bet, the pit boss walked over to spectate as the cards hit the table. The old woman and middle-aged man both glanced over, noticing the bet Daniel made on this lone hand. Daniel's first card was a six, while the old woman drew a king. The disgruntled man drew a five, bringing one more irritated reaction and the dealer placed her first card face-down. Next Daniel received a three, the woman a seven, and the man a two. Everyone watched attentively as the dealer placed a four on-top of the down card.

Daniel studied the cards as his heart rate raced and felt a flush of adrenaline come over him. He'd played plenty of blackjack in his life, so he knew what the correct play should be. *Push the boundaries of my life,* he thought as he looked at the dealer, smiled and said, "I'd like to double down, but I don't have the funds at the table."

The dealer called the pit boss over and Daniel explained his situation. "Do you have a credit or debit card?"

"Yes, I do," Daniel said. He reached into his wallet and handed his card to the man.

"Thank you. We'll charge the amount to your card. Feel free to continue your bet. If you win, we'll credit your card immediately."

"Thank you," Daniel said as the credit card was returned, and the festivities continued. Time seemed to slow to a halt as the dealer smiled at Daniel. "Good luck, sir."

She grabbed the next card and turned it over in front of Daniel. His brain, already flushed with a wave of dopamine, felt an immediate high as sitting on the table in front of him joining his other cards was the queen of hearts. He had nineteen, with the dealer sitting on a four. The old woman held and the man hit, receiving a ten for a total of seventeen. He also held there. Daniel started to sweat as the intensity thickened. All three players waited for the reveal of the dealer's hidden card. She took the four off and flipped the underneath card. It was a seven to the shock and disbelief of the players. Daniel felt his gut wrench as he waited for the dealer to take another card. A nine, ten or face card, and he loses. The next card was turned, revealing a three. The dealer sat on fourteen. Again, the players awaited the next card. Euphoria hit the table as the dealer revealed a jack and a bust. The dealer smiled and paid out their winnings. The pit boss pushed a credit receipt in front of Daniel. "Congratulations, sir. Here is your credit."

"Thank you," Daniel said, as he pushed a one-hundred-dollar chip in front of the dealer, picked up the rest of the chips and walked to the cash out window. Daniel returned to their room, climbed into bed, and instantly fell asleep, five-thousand dollars richer.

# Chapter Fourteen

D aniel and Madison returned home late Sunday evening. Madison's parents, who'd stayed the weekend with the children, welcomed them home with a late dinner of baked chicken. Emily and Logan were already in bed so they ate and talked about the trip before they said their goodbyes. Before bed, Daniel checked on each of his children who were both fast asleep. He felt a wave of pride and warmth as he looked at their innocent little faces. *They're growing up, creating their own identity,* Daniel thought as he closed Logan's door and headed to his own bedroom. *The circle of life continues to spin. Soon I'll be an old man and they'll have children of their own and they'll watch over them as they sleep with nostalgic, sentimental thoughts running through their own minds.*

Noticing Madison was already asleep, Daniel undressed, walked into the bathroom and looked in the mirror. His midsection had almost fully flattened. He noticed the outline of his uppermost abdomen muscles for the first time in fifteen years. His cheeks seemed to glow, his skin taut against the structure of is face. He could hardly detect the lines around his eyes and forehead. He glanced up at his hairline. The beginning of his widow's peak was less visible, partially filled in by thick, coarse hair.

"What the...?" he mumbled to himself. He looked in the mirror every day, but simply didn't notice the minute changes that seemed to progress over time. He rubbed his eyes, turned the bathroom light off, and climbed into bed. He was out moments after his head hit the pillow.


Daniel turned his back to the class and wrote:

*The real and effectual discipline which is exercised over a workman is that of his customers. It's the fear of losing their employment which restrains his frauds and corrects his negligence.*

He turned back towards his students and asked, "What does this sentence mean to you, the clever youth of America?"

Brian raised his hand.

"Brian, go ahead."

"It means people like money."

Laughter echoed through the class.

Daniel held up his hand. "Although Brian meant his response in a comical way, there is truth to what he said. People like money and are driven by compensation for their hard work and knowledge." Daniel pointed to the blackboard and continued. "That's a famous quote of Adam Smith, economist, philosopher, and the founding father of capitalism. One of Smith's observations was that production was enhanced by the assigning of specific tasks to individual workers. This division of labor would maximize production by allowing workers to specialize in certain aspects of the production process. He saw in the division of labor and in expanding markets virtually limitless possibilities for the expansion of wealth through manufacture and trade."

Daniel placed the chalk down and walked to the front of his desk, leaned back and continued. "He also held that individuals acting in their own self-interest would naturally seek out economic activities that provided the greatest financial rewards. Smith was convinced this self-interest would in turn maximize the economic well-being of society as a whole. He also argued that production and distribution of wealth could work most effectively in the absence of government interference. Such a *laissez-faire*, that is, 'leave alone', or 'allow to be' policy would, in his opinion, encourage the most efficient operation of private and commercial enterprises. He was not against government involvement in public projects too large for private investment, but rather objected to its meddling in the market mechanism. As such, the term 'Capitalism' was born."

Hands flew into the air when Daniel finished his synopsis. "Ah, I was expecting this type of reaction. It's of no secret this is a hot-button topic in our beloved country today. Stephanie, go ahead."

"Isn't capitalism at its core evil? I mean, profiting from the needs of others? Shouldn't we just help one another without expecting materialistic payments in return?"

"Maybe in a perfect, imaginary world where food falls from the clouds and clothing and shelter grow on trees. However, we share our world with seven-billion people and systems are needed to value food, materials, and services. Bartering and trading goes back eight thousand years, introduced to the world by the Mesopotamia tribes. The Phoenicians and Babylonians followed suite, developing and improving the bartering system. Today, of course, we use a monetary system which regulates a value to everything, however, the concept remains the same. One party gives money for a product of worth which is in turn used to purchase something else of worth to them, all the while trying to satisfy their trading partner's needs, or else they'll look elsewhere and give their business to a third party. It's all about balance and competition."

Julie raised he hand. "Yes, Julie?"

"I understand the concept of capitalism, and it may be needed on an economic scale, but I remember growing up with my mother and father never home because they were always working. They were trapped in the rat race. Learn, grow, work, work, work, retire, die. Surely we have less materialistic goals for a better life, a more peaceful life. Spending time with our friends and families is a better route, no?"

"Well, Julie, that question has a different answer for everyone. I'll say humans are driven by a competitive nature to work to be the best, accomplish the most, and attract the perfect mate. Those that grind the most create new medicines, invent devices and machines that make our lives more efficient, and find the answers to the world's greatest problems. However, that may not be everyone's goal. What is ultimately most important to you? We make our paths from the answers to that question. I think for most, a happy medium is what we strive to obtain."

He felt his cell in his pocket vibrate as the lecture came to an end.

"Okay, that's enough for today. Enjoy your evening. I'll see you all here tomorrow."

The students had all vacated the room so Daniel pulled out his cell and saw a new text from Tim.

*Got time for a drink?*

Daniel replied:

*Sure. 5 at Julienne's?*

Tim replied with a thumbs up. Daniel grinned. He hadn't entered the world of emoji's yet and found it humorous that a man of Tim's age used them. He wondered if that made him mature, or just old?

He pulled his cell back out and returned Tim's thumb with one of his own.

* * *

Daniel walked into to Julienne's and sat at the bar next to Tim, who looked to be on his second drink already.

"Here he is. How was Aruba?"

"Amazing." Daniel raised his hand to order his usual, scotch on the rocks. "The resort was perfect, the weather was beautiful, and Madison was happy to get away with me."

"A win, win, win."

"Exactly." Daniel paused as a memory shot through his head. "I have a little story for you."

"Go on, I've got all night."

"Friday night I couldn't sleep. Madison was out so I went to the casino to play a bit of blackjack."

"Hey, there's nothing wrong with a bit of gambling when you're on vacation, that's why the casino is there."

"Sure, however, dropping twenty-five hundred on one hand is something I would have never done before."

"Come again? "Tim blinked in surprise. "Twenty-five hundred? Tell me you won."

"I did. But where did that come from? I mean, I think I'm changing. I think these excursions are changing me. I feel younger, braver, without the fear and cowardice that usually overtakes me in those situations. Have you felt any different over the last five months?"

"Well, now that you mention it, I had a physical yesterday."

"Yeah, what's so strange about that?"

"Nothing other then my blood pressure and cholesterol have dropped some."

Daniel held a steady gaze at his friend. "Seriously? That's great Tim. "Have you changed your diet or started a new workout?"

"Nope, nothing."

"But that just doesn't make sense. Health issues don't just go away unless you change your habits."

Tim put his hands up and shrugged his shoulders as the bartender placed new drinks in front of them. "Thanks Paul," Tim said, as he dropped a five on the bar for a tip.

"Have you thought about our February getaway?"

"I've already decided."

"Well?"

Tim looked around as if the subject was a matter of national security. Daniel enjoyed these moments of drama that only Tim could seem to pull off. When Tim was finally convinced it was safe to discuss his secret, he turned back to Daniel and moved in a bit closer to his friend.

"Have you ever seen a manatee?"

"A manatee? You mean those creatures who look like a cross between a walrus and a dolphin?"

"Well, sure, if you happen to think that but it's not really accurate. Do you know manatees are related to elephants and the hyrax?"

"What the heck's a hyrax?"

"It's a furry, small herbivore, kinda resembles a guinea pig."

"So, a large, swimming creature that resembles a walrus is related to a rat?"

Tim looked at him with disappointment, like he totally missed out on the ecology course they had in science in school.

"Not rats, my friend, hyraxes. Totally different creature."

"Okay, I apologize to the hyraxes and the manatees. Are these creatures dangerous?"

"As gentle as a cow, or an elephant."

"So, what do manatees have to do with us and our next excursion?"

"We're going to swim with them."

"Say what? Are you out of your mind?"

"Really You want to veto manatees, you pussy?"

"No, I didn't say that, it's just...well..."

Tim waited for a response that never came.

"It's settled then, manatees it is."

Tim raised his thumb into the air in a mock gesture of Daniel's last text. They both had a short laugh then Daniel drained his drink and rose to leave.

"Hey, congrats on the blackjack hand. What's better than leaving a casino up twenty-five hundred?"

"It wasn't twenty-five I left with, it was five-grand. I doubled down," he said before turning and walking out.

# Chapter Fifteen

"But dad, aren't manatees dangerous?" asked Logan.

"No, son. They're like cows of the sea. Did you know they can swim in fresh or saltwater? Pass the green beans please, Emily."

"Aren't they really big?" Emily asked, as she handed Daniel the bowl of sautéed green beans.

"Sure, the adult males are one-thousand pounds or so. Thank you."

"Well, how do you know they won't accidentally crush you?"

Daniel shoveled a mouthful of beans into his mouth and chewed. Madison smiled as they all awaited his answer.

He swallowed and continued. "Sweetheart, I'll be in their territory. They maneuver in water better than we do on land. They won't crush me, I promise. Pass the roast, please."

Madison gave him an odd look as she handed over the plate of roast. "Daniel, what's gotten into you? You haven't eaten like this since we first met."

"Daniel paused to look at his plate, his second serving was almost completely consumed. "I don't know, just hungry, I guess. Maybe I'll look like a manatee when I visit them," he said, and he winked at his children who giggled in response.


"'There's only one really serious philosophical problem, and that is suicide,' so claims Albert Camus in his essay. *The Myth of Sisyphus*. By starting with the question of whether life is worth living, Camus places the problem of how we're to live our lives squarely in the center of his thought. He concludes that suicide is of little use to us, as there can be no more meaning in death than in life and turns to questions of what makes life worth living. Camus makes a rather bold claim on the meaning of life—there simply isn't one and we can't just create one either. He argues that it's impossible for us to find a satisfying answer to the question of the meaning of life, and any attempt to impose a meaning on the universe will end in disaster. He further denies that science, philosophy, society, or religion could ever create a meaning of life that would be immune to the problem of absurdity."

"Jesus, Mr. B., he sounds like a dude you'd want to invite to a party," Brian said. "He must have had loads of friends."

When the laughter died down, Daniel continued. "However, Camus didn't see this meaninglessness as bad. He explains that to understand that life is absurd is the first step to being fully alive. While the problem of living in a world devoid of meaning is a big one, it's one to be solved like any other. What makes life worth living then? He praised sunshine, women, the beach, dancing, and good food. He loved sports and was a champion soccer player in his youth. He took great enjoyment in the little things and encouraged us to do so as well. Just because life is meaningless doesn't mean it can't be enjoyed.

Indeed, the meaninglessness is just a background fact, like gravity, that must be reckoned with. It's no wonder then that Camus was an unbeliever."

Jennifer, a fourth-year student, raised her hand in obvious disgust.

"Go ahead, Jennifer."

"I don't understand atheists. I mean, why are they so intent on invading our faith, mocking us, and talking like our beliefs are absurd?"

"Well, Camus was humble about his beliefs. His own lack of faith did not presume that others must be wrong about theirs. For this reason, he chose the label *incroyant*, a French word meaning non-believer, or better known today as agnostic."

"But isn't that inherently a contradiction? I mean, you can't be a non-believer but still accept the reality that God may exist."

"Ah, and therein lies the crux of the problem of religion in our world. Someone *must* be wrong. You can't have evolution *and* Adam and Eve. However, there must always be a certain amount of respect for the beliefs of others, for if there is one thing that Socrates has taught us, my wonderful students, that would be?"

Half the class responded in unison, "The only thing I know for certain, is that I know nothing."

Daniel clapped his hands. "You all get ten points extra credit on your next test. We'll end this class on that fine note. Have a great day and a wonderful, safe weekend."

The class filed out of the room, buzzing from the generous offering of their teacher. One student remained seated, however. When the room was empty, Jennifer stood and approached Daniel's desk.

"What can I help you with, Jennifer?"

"Mr. Burton, are you a non-believer?"

Daniel sat back, felt the coarse stubble on his chin and answered, "I don't really know that answer, Jennifer. At times I have and at times I haven't. I'd like to think we have a higher power guiding us, helping us, welcoming us into an afterlife of love and peace, however, my analytical mind and cynical attitude towards certain aspects of history give me doubts. Why are you so certain that you believe?"

Jennifer looked a bit uncomfortable. She was always a good student, but quick to stay in the shadows and not open up about the many discussions of life brought forth in his classroom. Daniel saw the flash in her eyes the moment she decided to take a chance and engage on the subject further.

"It was four years ago, the January before my first year here. I had scheduled a trip to Florida with my best friend, Katie. I received a call the night before the flight from a man with a deep, smooth voice. He said, 'Jennifer Stanton? This is Christian Adler from LaGuardia Airport. I'm sorry to inform you that your flight #178 has been cancelled due to maintenance issues. We can transfer you to flight #195, which departs at 10:00 am, two hours later.'

"I remember being silent for a moment, and then accepting the transfer. I mean, what could I do? Obviously, the change was to protect me, and I already had reservations scheduled for the weekend and it was only a two-hour delay, so I agreed and arrived at the airport at 8:45, hoping to take care of any paperwork needed for the transfer. When I arrived, the agent informed me that I had missed my flight, that it had departed on time. I informed her of the call, how Mr. Christian had known all my information about me and the flight. She informed me that there was no record of the call, or of any transfer. She could, however, get me on flight #195, with an added fee which I would have to absorb. I was furious. I told her to contact Mr. Christian and get to the bottom of the confusion. She typed a few things into her computer and this strange expression came over her. She looked at me and said, 'Ms. Carson, I'm sorry but we have no record of a Mr. Christian here. He doesn't work for us. Are you sure you have the correct name?'"

Jennifer paused to take in Daniel's reaction up to this point. Daniel gave her a slight nod of his head, gesturing her to continue.

"He was a mystery man. No one there by that name."

Suddenly her eyes teared up and she turned away for a moment to gather herself. When she continued, her voice was soft and subdued.

"We finally came to an agreement and I was scheduled on the second flight. Shortly after, hell broke loose. Flight #178 had crashed into the Atlantic Ocean."

Daniel took a deep breath understanding the seriousness of Jennifer's story.

"I remember that," he said. "Tragic, one-hundred and three died. Are you telling me *that* flight was supposed to be yours?"

She slowly nodded her head as tears fell freely.

"I searched for Christian Adler everywhere. On the internet, made calls on the phone, nothing. No sign of the man at all."

Daniel watched as she continued, starting to understand what she was implying.

"I know it sounds strange, but I believe Mr. Christian was an angel sent from God to save my life. It's the only explanation."

"Jennifer, you have every right to your own beliefs, and I wouldn't begin to try to discount you story. Faith is different for everyone. It's like ice cream. You may like chocolate while I love vanilla. Someone else may believe pistachio or black cherry is the best. We all have the right to our own taste and beliefs in life. If your belief in God and Mr. Adler makes you a happier person, than who am I to dispute it?"

"Did you really just compare God to an ice cream flavor?" She then gave Daniel a hug, whispered *thank you* in his ear and walked out of the classroom.


Daniel gazed out of the window as the plane made its descent into the Crystal River, Florida airport. The view was nothing short of amazing. The late morning sunshine sparkled off the water as they slowly inclined toward the beautiful landscape below. The solid ground was segregated by countless canals and inlets which were as blue as the sky above. Daniel felt a charge of adrenaline as the plane crept toward land. He turned and glanced at Tim, who was also captivated by the show of nature in front of them. Ten minutes later, they were safely on the ground and retrieving their luggage.

"Ready for this?" Tim asked as they made their way to their waiting rental car.

"If I can ride a bull, I can swim with manatees. You, on the other hand, can't ride a bull."

They threw their bags in the backseat, jumped into the vehicle with Tim behind the wheel, and headed for their hotel.

The following day they woke early, stopped for breakfast at a local diner, and headed to meet their guide, a woman named Angelica, then board bus that would take them to Three Sisters Springs where the manatees flock to each winter.

"The town and its surrounding waters are filled with natural springs that remain a warm seventy-two degrees year-round, drawing in the manatees that can't survive in colder water. Some never leave, keeping residence in these balmy springs," Angelic said as the bus passed through a small town and into the swampy, tropical wilderness. They drove through several inlets before coming to a stop at Three Sisters Springs. They exited the vehicle and followed the guide to a series of docks overlooking a spring.

"Wow, that looks amazing," Daniel said as they took in the crystal clear, azure water from the dock.

"See there," Angelica said, pointing across the water. "A pair of manatees are basking in the sun, their backs just breaking the surface."

"Holy shit, they're big," Tim said.

"They're a couple of youngsters. They get much bigger than that."

Tim glanced at Daniel with his eyebrows raised which brought a small shrug of the shoulders from Daniel.

"We're going to don some snorkels. I know you both have experience, but I'll take fifteen minutes to give you a refresher and then we'll take a pontoon boat from which we'll enter the water and the world of these wonderful creatures."

After a quick lesson on snorkeling, they boarded the boat and headed west toward an area the manatees were known to haunt. In a matter of minutes, they spotted two manatees just below the water. The Captain stopped the boat as the duo slowly glided toward them. They used their paddle-like tails to propel themselves up and down. The manatees steered with their flippers, gracefully moving their twelve-foot long bodies through the water. Soon, the boat was soon surrounded by this gentle species. Angelica then gave Daniel and Tim instructions. "Whatever you do, remember the three golden rules. Minimize splash noise, act with very slow movements, and when you do touch one of these friendly gentle gray giants on the back or stomach, never touch with more than one hand at a time. Two hands are illegal."

It was time to take the plunge and visit these animals in their home. Daniel gave one last glance toward Tim and gave him a wink. They entered the water very slowly, trying not to disturb the manatees and also trying to keep down the amount of sediment rising from the bottom of the river. Upon their descent, some of the manatees were still sleeping while others were paddling around slowly. Daniel sunk down, amazed by the cerulean color of the water. Daniel remembered stepping outside his home during a snow-storm and entering a different world; a winter-wonderland. This experience created the same effect. He entered a new world, a world he'd never visited.

The sun's rays shot through the crystal blue water, creating a beauty he'd never witnessed, an obscure beauty of nature that makes you paralyzed in awe of what your eyes are seeing. Suddenly, a large manatee glided over and settled a few feet from Daniel. He looked the creature in the eyes and felt a chill as the manatee stared right back at him, their eyes locked in a gaze of curiosity and respect. It wasn't just man and animal, it was the feeling of two kindred souls joined together by our crazy world, in a crazy universe. Daniel reached out one hand slowly and waited to gauge the manatee's reaction. The gentle giant just waited, still holding Daniel's gaze. He reached further until his hand felt the soft, silky smooth skin and began petting the creature's back. Daniel noticed the look in its eyes. The warmth, affection, and happiness. He felt a kinship with the creature and suddenly realized all living things are connected in some cosmic, omnipresent way, and our universal language should always be love.

They rode the boat back to the dock in silence. Nothing needed to be said as they had both experienced something as deep and crucial as life itself, and silently, Daniel wondered how anyone could kill any animal, any living thing, now having felt the limitless connection two living things on opposite ends of the world could share. Later that evening as they lay in bed, Daniel broke the silence.

"Nothing I've ever experienced or witnessed before could have prepared me for that experience. I have a new respect for every species we share this planet with."

Tim didn't respond for a bit, brooding over the memory, until he finally spoke. "A couple drifted over to me, with the larger—the male—leading the way. What I can only assume was once he felt comfortable, he allowed his mate to come forward. After a period of time of us building each other's trust and confidence, their calf came forward. But I didn't touch him like I did the parents. I just watched him, and he watched me under the close supervision of the mother. How friendly and loving are these creatures to trust me enough to let that happen? There's so much people could learn from these wonderful animals."

They fell asleep, their souls purified, their faith of the world restored, and will to live revitalized.

# Chapter Sixteen

Daniel pulled his shirt over his head as he waited for Doctor Walker to enter the room. He started to become restless as he had a class scheduled for 1:00 PM, just ninety minutes away. Suddenly the door flew open and the doctor energetically walked in and held out his hand to Daniel.

"Mr. Burton, so nice to see you. Any issues, complaints, or concerns?"

"No, I feel great, actually."

"Perfect, and your tests came out excellent. Blood pressure couldn't be better, heart rate is perfect, and I see you've dropped a few pounds. Have you stated a new diet? Workout?"

"No, nothing."

The doctor looked up from his chart. "Nothing has changed? Are you sure? I mean, a man of your age just doesn't become healthier without an attempt to accomplish it."

"Nothing consciously has changed. I eat the same, maybe a bit more, actually."

"And you don't exercise?"

"No, well, nothing like a workout. I've become more active. Went bull riding recently. Ziplining. You know, just enjoying nature and life a bit more."

"Well, that must be it. Whatever you are doing, keep it up, my friend."

The doctor scribbled on a piece of paper and handed it to Daniel. "This is for bloodwork next door. You can check your results online in a few days or so. If all is good, I'll see you next year."

They shook hands and the doctor walked out.

Daniel completed the bloodwork and headed to school to teach his next class.


Daniel waited, seated at his desk, for his full body of students to arrive, settle down, and give him their full attention. When he thought the time right to start the lecture, he stood and walked to the windows overlooking the courtyard and glanced out as he began.

"What are your thoughts on torture used to acquire information?"

He then turned to face his students.

"Don't be shy people, tell us what you think and feel about it."

"I think it's evil," said an attractive first year student, as she looked around the room for support from her colleagues.

"I agree," chimed in a young man who donned a spike through his nose and two gauges in his ears. "Using violence to gain information is never a positive choice."

Daniel shook his head to insinuate he understood their stance.

"Have you ever heard of the term thought experiment? No? Well I'm going to introduce one to you now. This thought experiment is called the 'ticking bomb problem,' which asks us to put ourselves in a very difficult, slippery situation as follows." Daniel ticked off on his fingers.

"A terrorist group states that it has concealed a nuclear bomb in New York.

"The authorities have captured the leader of the group.

"He says that he knows where the bomb is.

"He refuses to reveal the location.

"Torture is guaranteed to produce the information needed to ensure the authorities find and make the bomb safe. So, my intelligent righteous, morally pure libertarians, what do you do?"

Silence engulfed the room.

"The most virtuous people face a problem when thinking about torture. Is there ever a case when a good result produced by torture justifies the evil act? An answer which focuses on the reality of the ethical situation might say that one, it's unethical to torture the terrorist. Two, it's also unethical to let your moral principles condemn thousands of others to an avoidable death. Three, so in this case, there's no ethically acceptable course of action; whatever you do is morally wrong. Four, it's understandable, but still wrong, for the interrogators to torture the terrorist in this case to save lives, and five, sometimes an ethically wrong act can be forgiven, in this case because it is a perfectly intelligible human choice to make.

"What if thousands of innocent people will die, some of them children and even babies. Is it still considered evil or morally negative? By the way, it's important to understand that this answer does not justify the decision to torture, nor does it argue that we are justified in choosing the least bad option. Instead it should be interpreted rather differently. Here are a couple of ways of doing it. Torturing the terrorist is unethical and can't be justified, but it can be understood, and it can be forgiven. Torturing the terrorist is unethical, but in those circumstances, it's the 'right thing to do'. This is not intellectually satisfactory and I'm by no means trying to tell you torturing anyone is acceptable, but it does acknowledge that hard cases can't always be solved in a neat way. The world isn't always as black and white as we'd like it to be, and sometimes the answers aren't easy to discover. Sometimes we need to look closer at the subject matter in question, at the shadowy depths that hide many truths and realities."

After class, Julie stood by Daniel's desk as Michael walked in, hugged Julie and greeted Daniel with a handshake.

"Mr. Burton, I want to thank you for giving me a chance and helping me receive the help I needed. Julie and I are happier now more than ever."

"Julie, do you agree with Michael? Are you happy?"

"I am, Mr. Burton. Michael sees his therapist every week and he's changed. He's more understanding, gentle even, with a new-found patience. We want to get married after we graduate."

"I'm glad to hear it. Michael, you must continue to get help. The issues you had can, and frequently do, come back. If you truly love her, you must see this through. However, I'm proud of you. I talk to Jason often and he's very positive and content with the recovery you've made. Please keep up the good work, son."

Daniel shook hands with Michael and watched the couple walk out, happily holding hands. He smiled, packed up his briefcase, locked the door, and headed home.

# Chapter Seventeen

The month sleepily crept by as only February in the northeast can. Daniel always said, although it was the shortest month by measurement of time, the mental act of living through it in that part of the country seemed to play tricks on people's perception of time. What was a short four weeks felt disguised as eight weeks when you had to live through it in the North.

Another storm blasted New York and New Jersey leaving a foot and a half of fresh snow on top of the frozen remnants of a previous storm. That was the process: snow then cold, turning the fluffy powder to a hard, packed, surface of ice. Rinse and repeat, over and over again.

It was a Saturday after a late Friday blizzard which crippled most of the area but giving Daniel an opportunity to spend the day with his children without interruptions. They started the day skating on a nearby pond, frozen to its core, then went to some nearby hills to sled and finished off the outing in the early evening building snow forts and having a snowball fight in the yard. The children were the first to tire, asking to head in for hot chocolate and a movie. Daniel watched his children sipping the hot chocolate wrapped in blankets as the movie started and thought, *Is there any better feeling in the world for a child?*

After the movie ended, Daniel put the children to bed and walked into the bedroom to a nude Madison waiting for him. They made love intensely, with Daniel displaying the energy of a man half his age. A short few moments after finishing, Daniel was ready for a second session, his erection fully erect and hungry once again.

"What the hell has gotten into you?" Madison asked as Daniel entered her.

The second round was everything the first was and more, sending Madison off into multiple realms of pleasure until she lay exhausted and content.

"Where the hell do you get the energy, sweetheart? You were out all day, aren't you tired?" she said, laying her head on his chest.

"No, I feel great."

Madison lifted her head to look at her husband, rose and walked over to her dresser opening a drawer to grab something then returned to bed. She handed a photograph to him.

"I remember this photo. We were at the beach, the summer before Emily was born."

"Correct. Look at it. Tell me what you see."

"Well, it's a younger me."

"Yes, a younger you, but now ten years later you look the same."

"Why, thank you, Maddie, but I'm far from the same...visually or mentally."

"Oh, really? Have you seen yourself lately? Tighter, smoother, taught skin, a youthful sparkle in your eye. Daniel, what's going on? I'd ask you if you were having an affair, but I know you wouldn't do that, so what is it?"

"I have no idea and honestly haven't noticed. I mean, I know I've lost a few pounds, but I've been extremely active the last year. I'm happy, Madison. Certainly, there's nothing wrong with that."

"No, of course not."

They drifted off to sleep with the February winds whipping against their window and the chill in the air, countered by the fusion of their bodies wrapped together, keeping them warm.


On his way to school the following day, a song played he hadn't heard in almost thirty years. As he drove down the highway settling into a comfortable speed, he was transported to back to memories of his life that were connected to the music on the radio. It was a recollection of his first girlfriend, Avery Hayden, an innocent, intelligent, fair-haired girl who was the epitome of the American girl next door. It just so happened that she did live next door, residing directly across from Daniel on Misty River Lane. Daniel wasn't just daydreaming, he was actually transported back in time, remembering their first kiss. He felt the softness of her skin, her natural, wholesome scent, the soft innocence of her lips as they met his and she opened her eyes to glance at him, in a humble gesture to gauge if she was doing it correctly.

The song ended and Daniel was pulled out of his recollection. He was amazed by how real the moment felt and wondered just what the connection was with music and our brains that made it so authentic. It wasn't just a memory, it was re-living the moment, all brought on by some notes and lyrics, creating a magically portal in our hearts and minds.

Daniel pulled into the teachers parking lot and headed into his room as his text tone went off, revealing a message from Tim.

*Drinks tonight? I'm eager to hear about March's excursion.*

Daniel entered his room, placed his briefcase down on his desk and answered:

*I have decided. Julienne's at six.*

Daniel walked into a busy and hectic night at the bar which was common in the northeast in February. People yearn to get out at least for a short while and a drink can warm the insides as a stubborn winter refuses to yield. Tim was already present, apparently discussing some very serious topics to a group of three young attractive women. He was extremely animated as his hands flailed and he spoke with vigor and passion. As Daniel approached, Tim waved him over and pointed. The youthful beauties turned to look, each sporting an eager smile.

"Hello, partner," Tim said as Daniel sat beside him on the far end of the ladies. "Meet Abby, Gillian, and Kora." Tim motioned for the bartender to grab Daniel his favorite drink.

Daniel held out his hand to each. "Ladies, so nice to meet you."

"Likewise," Kora said with a brilliant smile. Daniel noticed her charmingly timid pale blue eyes and her straight, shiny, ebony hair. Daniel thought it an amazing visual contrast and felt a slight sexual reaction surface that he quickly pushed away.

"You must be the philosophy teacher," the blonde-haired, green-eyed goddess said as she took his hand.

"One in the same," Daniel replied. "Nice to make your acquaintance...?" his eyes asked a question as he spoke.

"Gillian," she smiled with a sexy confidence, holding Daniel's glance just a bit too long as he turned to the final woman.

"And you must be Abby." The bartender placed Daniel's drink in front of him, quickly glancing from Daniel to Abby and back again.

"Yes, and you're the famous Daniel."

"Well, I wouldn't say famous, but unrelentingly popular works."

She laughed and Daniel thought she was the most attractive of the group. She didn't have the sexy, intense contrast of Kora, or the classic beauty of Gillian, but she had a mysterious, demure disposition that he found enticing and felt the challenge of uncovering more. He felt transported to his college days of chasing and exploring women. He quickly turned back to Tim, hoping his friend would get the odd glance and message behind it, but Tim kept talking.

"So, how old are you guys?" Gillian asked, obviously the most aggressive of the trio.

"We are in our mid-forties," Tim replied.

"What? Are you shitting me? You both look like you're in your early thirties."

"Nope, but thank you," Tim said.

"Are you married?"

"Yes, I am, but Romeo here isn't." He noticed Abby glance his way as he uncovered his confession.

"Will you ladies be around for a while? Daniel and I have some business to take care of, but I'll be here after."

*So, he did get the meaning of my glance,* Daniel thought.

"Sure, we'll be around. It's our weekly night out together. Come by later on," Gillian said.

Daniel watched as the three walked away to the back of the bar and sat at a table in the corner.

"How old are they?"

"Mid-twenties."

"Are you crazy? They could be our daughters."

"I don't have a problem with that, old man," Tim said with a chuckle.

Daniel wiped a few beads of sweat off his forehead and decided to change the subject. "We're going to jump out of an airplane."

Tim looked from Daniel to the trio of beauties and back at Daniel again. "Say what?"

"It's called Above the Poconos. It's in Pennsylvania."

"I know where it is, but skydiving? This is a notch up for us, no?"

"A notch up from riding a bull or swimming with a one-ton animal? Naaaa..."

Tim ran his fingers through his hair.

"Doesn't matter anyway, only I have veto power."

Tim felt his chin and replied, "Okay, bigshot, skydiving it is." He lifted his glass in salute to his lifelong friend. Daniel countered with his own.

"To life, us, and young, beautiful women," Tim said as he stole another glance at the females.

Daniel followed his gaze and shook his head.

# Chapter Eighteen

February finally surrendered to March and the weather responded with the first few signs of spring breaking through the cold, grey skies. Daniel turned his face to the sun's warm rays as he strolled up the walkway to enter Princeton. It was the first Friday in March and he and Tim would be leaving the next day for Pennsylvania. His excitement had been building all week and he found it challenging to keep his mind on anything but Saturday. He entered his office and sat down, wondering what jumping out of a plane from fifteen thousand feet feels like. There was still thirty minutes before the start of his first class of the day, Philosophy 110, so he fired up his laptop and started to plan some future lessons. Moments later, Susan Gomes walked in and Daniel glanced up, surprised to see a student so early. Instead of taking her seat, she marched up to his desk.

"Hello, Susan. What can I do for you?"

"Hi, Mr. Burton." She looked around uneasily, finding it hard to hold his glance. "I have to tell you something that's very hard for me to say."

Daniel pushed his laptop aside and gave her his full attention. "Go on."

"I have to drop out of school."

"What? Why?"

Daniel noticed her eyes water as she continued. "My father has cancer. Gilosarcoma. It's a rare brain cancer and he needs special treatment which isn't fully covered by his medical coverage. We can't afford to pay my tuition and I need to work to help my mother pay the medical bills." The watery eyes had let go and now tears streamed freely down her cheeks. Daniel rose and walked over to her. He held her in his arms and patted her back, ignoring one of the golden rules of being a teacher: never touch your students.

"Susan, I'm so sorry."

Her sobs eased and Daniel released her, pointed to her desk and said, "Have a seat."

She sat in the first desk of the third row, where she'd called home throughout her time in his class.

"Susan, I know I don't have to inform you how important education is, and not just because of the money you'll make or the prestige you'll receive from a Princeton diploma and a high-profile career. Education is the ability to think and apply those thoughts to the world. It's a direct link to understanding the value of life. You, Susan, are one of the students who can make a difference in this world. Solve problems, help others, change the future. You have that intelligence, drive, and ability. Your education is your passport to your future."

"I understand you, Mr. Burton, however I don't have a choice in this matter. I must make this decision for my family."

Daniel paced the room, brooding over Susan and her situation. Finally, he came to rest, leaning against the desk next to hers.

"What if there was a way I could help you? Not just with your tuition, but with the medical bills?"

"No, I will not take a handout from you."

"Not a handout. Listen, give me two weeks. Continue to come to school, keep up your studies, put the job-hunt aside. If after the two weeks you're not satisfied with my offer, go forward with your plan."

Susan looked him in the eyes trying to decipher just what he had in mind.

Daniel smiled. "Deal?"

"Deal," she replied.

"Good." He walked back to his desk and sat down as other students started to file in, ready to shape their minds in a way that would prepare them for the rest of their lives.

That night Daniel prepared an email to a group of colleagues who were members on the board for the P.P.G. or the Princeton Professors Grant, a full ride grant given to a student who just needs a break, an opportunity, to attend Princeton. The recipient is chosen by majority vote from a board of professors who look at five candidates, all from different backgrounds and ethnicities. He wrote:

Dear members of the board,

I've recently uncovered a new candidate for the PPG. I'd like to formally apply her candidacy with the complete paperwork required at our next meeting on March 10. This is a unique situation and the candidate doesn't fit the usual profile for this grant. I urge you all to keep an open mind through this process.

Thank you,
Professor Daniel Burton

Daniel looked the email over one last time before hitting the send button. He then created a fund on social media in the name of Susan Gomes and her ill father. He was the first deposit, adding one thousand dollars to the fund. He then shared it with anyone and everyone he was connected to. Instantly, the fund started to grow as friends, family and acquaintances made deposits on his behalf. Everything was in motion. Now he just needed to convince the other four members of the board that Susan deserved the grant.

That night, Daniel lay awake in bed as his mind raced. His speech in front of the board supporting Susan as the right choice would be crucial. Strangely, the thought that he'd be jumping out of a plane from fifteen thousand feet hardly crossed his mind.

"Daniel, what's wrong?" Madison said as she turned over and put her hand on his chest.

"How'd you know something was bothering me?" he asked.

"I know when you can't sleep. You huff and puff just like the wolf trying to blow down the little pig's house."

"Sorry, it's that obvious?"

Madison slowly shook her head up and down.

"It's the Susan Gomes issue. I need to convince them she is the right choice. She needs this. Her life is at a crossroads and where she ends up will be a direct result of this grant."

"Daniel, all you can do is your best. Have some faith in your colleagues, I'm sure they respect and value your opinion and will make the best choice."

"This grant is usually earmarked for a minority with a rags-to-riches story that Princeton can use to support its liberal standings."

"Is that what the board is concerned about?"

"Well, no, but they'll get pressure from above."

"Daniel, trust in your colleagues and get some sleep," she said with a smile.

Daniel knew it wouldn't be that easy, but just discussing the issue with his wife helped to relax him. He fell asleep and dreamt of cancer patients jumping out of an airplane being piloted by Susan Gomes.


The world looks far different from a small plane at sixteen thousand feet. It's basically an orgy of geometric shapes colored with earth tones of blues, browns, and greens.

They had arrived at the Poconos Airport after the short flight from Newark, checked into a hotel room and grabbed a taxi to the skydiving center. After a few training drills and instructions, they were on their way, climbing into the Pennsylvania sky, finally reaching the desired height of sixteen thousand feet.

"Much different than a commercial flight?" one of the dive-instructor said as the plane steadied for the last run over the mountains before they jumped.

"It looks amazing," Daniel said as the plane banked to the left. They all held on until the plane finally leveled off heading west.

"Okay, Tim and I will jump first. Twenty seconds until we depart," Tim's dive-companion said.

"Once they jump, we follow, five seconds after."

Daniel swallowed hard and glanced at Tim, their eyes connecting one last time before the dive. Tim looked like he was about to vomit, his face a pale white and his eyes filled with uncertainty as they gazed out the open door through the googles. Then, suddenly, he was gone.

"Ready, three, two, one...!"

Then, nothing—and everything.

Daniel was experiencing so many things at once it was hard to separate one from another. Oddly, the first of his senses to take over was scent. He'd never smelled air so crisp, so clean, as it traveled through his sinuses at one-hundred miles-per-hour. He heard the loud rush of wind similar to the loud sound you hear the moment you splash into water. He felt the temperature change, it suddenly feeling much colder as the air pressure pushed against his body. Once he became accustomed to the changes, he opened his eyes wide and looked down. The beauty and detail he noticed was the most vivid he'd ever seen. Daniel felt freedom, bliss, focus, ands the confidence of having overcome his fears. Surprisingly, there were no G-forces like you feel on a rollercoaster. His stomach stayed with him the whole time. Daniel felt the instructor strapped in behind him look around and take in every aspect of the jump and Daniel realized no matter how many jumps you've done, it will always be a breathtaking experience.

Suddenly the chute opened, and Daniel felt a quick shot of regret for he could have free-fallen for another hour and still not believed how amazing it felt. Things became much calmer as they settled in, floating under the open chute. What moments ago was an intense, one-hundred-fifty miles per hour free-fall swiftly became a tranquil, scenic glide towards the ground. Tree-tops, lakes, open fields of green grass, all came into focus as they drifted toward earth. Daniel's thoughts surprising turned to society. All the technology in the world, one-thousand-dollar cell-phones, three-thousand-dollar computers, billion-dollar-budget movies, and nothing could come close to the experience that only nature could offer for free.

Moments later, the jump was over and Daniel was relieved to be safely on land, but also sorrowful that it was over. The instructor unstrapped him and he walked over to Tim who had landed a few seconds before him. The look on his friend's face was all he had to see. Tim had a frantic intensity in his eyes. Daniel stuck out his hand and as the two life-long friends shook, Tim pulled him in for a hug, letting Daniel know this was an experience he'd never forget.


Daniel returned home the following day and was back in the classroom the next, however, the life-altering experience of jumping out of the plane was hardly ever far from his mind and felt a renewed passion toward his life as a husband, father, and teacher.

"Has anyone ever heard of Roko's Basilisk?" Daniel searched the room for a face exhibiting any recognition of the phrase. "No one? Roko's Basilisk is a thought experiment about the potential risks involved in developing artificial intelligence. Imagine that at some point in the distant future, a super-A.I. comes into being that's capable of accurately simulating individual people from its past. So, if it were somehow aware of your existence, the A.I. could, at will, create a simulation of you accurate enough that the simulation would think it really *was* you."

Daniel paused and checked to make sure the whole class was still with him. He continued:

"Given that premise, next assume that this A.I. wants to incentivize humans in its past, our present, to bring it into being, in our future. One approach that it could take is as follows; identify every person in history who was aware of the potential for such an A.I. and determine whether each of them devoted their lives to making this A.I. a reality. If the A.I. judges that a given person didn't try hard enough then as punishment, it creates ten thousand simulations of that person and tortures them all in the most awful ways that it can devise."

Susan Gomes raised her hand.

"Yes, Susan?"

"Isn't that a paradox? I mean, if you truly believe that an accurate simulation *is* you, then you have an immense incentive to avert that potential torture, and thus you'll choose to devote your life to the creation of this evil super A.I., thereby aiding in your own cyber-driven prison."

"Excellent theory, Susan. That's exactly what makes Roko's Basilisk so confusing and counter-intuitive to us. By securing our safety, we're actually sealing our fate. The name 'Basilisk' reflects the essential point that it's only dangerous if you 'look it in the eye'. If you see it, it sees you and if it sees you, you're already doomed. Now, is this type of technology alive today? Probably not, however the government is working on many technological advances which are hardly known by the public. Who knows the progress being made with A.I.? At some point, this crazy, seemingly futuristic, sci-fi thought experiment may really come to fruition. Some day in our future we may be run by the same technological advances we've created to make our lives easier. The irony is never-ending."

Daniel finished up the lecture and headed home. The family had plans to get dinner and go bowling that evening and he looked forward to spending quality time with is wife and children. As he exited his car a brisk wind assaulted him, and he recoiled against the bitterness of the cold. As was usually the case in March in the northeast, winter was not yet ready to surrender to the warm sun of springtime. He walked into a warm house filled with the buzz of excited children in anticipation of a night out filled with fun and good times.

They arrived at the lanes, donned their bowling shoes, and took turns rolling the large marble spheres down the pine alleys, knocking down as many maple hourglass shaped objects as they could.

*How odd some of human's past-times can be,* Daniel thought as he rolled his first attempt down the lane, recording his first strike of the evening.

"Yay, Dad!" Logan cheered, as he tossed another strike on his next attempt.

An hour later he'd completed his two best games ever, scoring two-hundred-thirty and two-hundred-forty-two. Sitting at dinner, Madison touched on his improved technique.

"How did you get so much better? Did you take lessons I don't know about?"

Daniel smiled as his family waited for his response.

"To be honest, my knee had no pain at all. I can't remember the last time it felt this well. Without that hinderance, I felt free to use my natural form." He shrugged his shoulders. "That's it, really. I only bowl with you guys."

"Well, that's great, honey, but how can it suddenly be healed? You've always had discomfort."

"I have no idea," he answered, although he was starting to get a pretty good idea why.


Daniel sat in a conference room with the full P.P.G. board in attendance. He stood and shuffled to the front of the room.

"I nominate Susan Gomes for this grant. Susan is a perspicacious, intensely hard-working young woman who has recently fallen on extremely difficult times which demand some impossible decisions to be made. He father has recently fallen ill with Gilosarcoma, which causes a major financial burden on his family. He was the main source of the funds to pay for her tuition. Susan's plan is to quit school and get a job to help support her family. Now, I know what this young lady has to offer the world. Not only would it be a tragedy for her to discontinue her studies, it would be a disservice to the world. I believe there are great things in her future. Now, I realize she doesn't fit the usual profile for this grant. She isn't a minority, nor has she migrated from another country looking for an opportunity to achieve. She comes from a lower-middle class family. There is no rags-to-riches story here to sell to the powers that be or the press. However, this is a case that set the example of why these types of grants were created in the first place. She is a special person who just needs some help—and help, my colleagues, is what we are here for."

Daniel paced a bit searching for just the right words to leave an impact, stopping at the head of the conference table and pausing to create the perfect mood.

"Ladies and gentlemen, this is why we teach. Susan Gomes is exactly the reason we sign our bloated contracts, show up when it's snowing and twenty degrees out. She's what we all dream of as a student. Someone who, with our proper guidance and support, will become someone who makes a difference. That, my friends, I guarantee will happen with Susan if we just give her the chance."

Daniel paused to let his speech sink in.

"Any questions?"

Professor West asked, "Even if she were to receive this grant, how do we know she won't drop out anyway to help her family cope with the bills?"

"I've already put some things in motion to rectify that issue."

"As in?" Professor Ernst asked.

"I've created a fund in her name. I have printouts for you which I'll now pass out. On them, you will see the amount I have raised in just over a week."

The panel all read the amount and were satisfied.

"We can and will make this work. All I need is your help, your vote for Susan, and we can change a life together."

# Chapter Nineteen

Daniel entered Tim's apartment and sat on the couch without uttering a word. The time had come to bring the secrets into the open. Tim walked behind his bar.

"Drink?"

"Sure."

"Your usual?"

"That's fine."

He returned, handed Daniel his scotch and sat beside him.

Daniel took a sip, placed the glass on the table in front of him and began.

"I've lost weight without changing my diet or exercise habits. My wrinkles have faded, my resting heartrate has dropped, my hair is thicker, and my knee issues have all but disappeared."

Tim watched as Daniel continued his rant.

"My doctor says I'm healthier than I've been in years. Seriously, look at us Tim. We both look ten years younger."

"Why is that a problem? What's wrong with looking or feeling younger?"

"Tim, be honest. What has your doctor said about you?"

"He says my blood pressure has dropped to the point that I don't require antihypertensives anymore."

"Is that normal? A middle-aged man with a history of high blood pressure just 'all of a sudden' is cured?"

"No, he was pretty perplexed by the whole thing. Even so, what's wrong with it? I'm healthier, feel and look younger...you act like it's a negative."

"It's just alarming, is all. We don't know how or why. If we've somehow found a way to halt the aging process, don't you think we should be studied? What if there are side-affects we don't know about or have uncovered yet? If or when they do rise to the surface will we even understand them?"

Tim sighed and finished off his drink. He walked behind the bar to pour another, raising the bottle to Daniel.

"No, I'm good," Daniel said, responding to Tim's gesture. Tim returned to his seat.

"How do we even know why this is happening? Are you convinced it's a result of our expeditions?"

"What else could it be? What else is different about our lives?"

Tim looked away. "I don't know."

"Doesn't it worry you, the abnormality of it all? Don't you want some answers?"

"I don't need answers for feeling and looking like I'm ten years younger. Who wouldn't want that? Are you telling me you're out?"

Daniel sighed and finished off his scotch. "No, but if this continues, I'll revisit the thought."

Tim smiled. "Good, cause I have a great idea for the next one."

Daniel put up his hand. "Next week. Julienne's on Wednesday. I need some time to think first."

"Okay, next week it is."

Daniel walked out feeling like he hadn't made any progress in getting through to his friend.


Susan Gomes kept her word and continued to come to class and study with an energetic vigor which Daniel had become accustomed to. He smiled at his favorite student as he began his lecture.

"Today, my geniuses, I'd like to discuss the importance of a subject which has been feared in our society by many from the beginning of thought. Mathematics. Shakuntala Devi once said, 'Without mathematics, there's nothing in this world you can do.' Everything around you is based on mathematics, everything. Numbers are everywhere."

Daniel walked over to crack a window as the first hint of spring had fallen over the late March New Jersey sky. He paused and let the fresh, crisp air fill his lungs.

Albert Einstein said, 'Pure mathematics is the poetry of logical ideas.' Who present here today cringe at the thought of mathematics, algebra, geometry, trigonometry, and calculus?"

All students but two raised their hands.

"Susan and Tom, you didn't raise your hands. Do you enjoy mathematics, and if so, why?"

"I wouldn't say I like it, it just always seemed to come easy to me," Tom said.

"Well be happy for that talent, Tom. Most struggle with its theories and concepts. Susan?"

"I don't know, it's always just made sense to me. I agree with Einstein. I think there's an endless beauty in numbers and the way they interact. Aside from that, all those branches of math you have listed are simply based on logic. It all makes perfect sense, unlike other courses such as language and history." Susan shrugged her shoulders. "I guess I'm just left side of the brain dominant."

"Very well stated, Susan. Us lefties are few and far between, but we're out there," Daniel said with a smile. "Mathematics is constantly present in nature and our universe is literally made from mathematics in the same way that computer programs are made out of a series of construct code. Let's discuss some examples of how our world is constructed by numbers."

Daniel walked to the blackboard and wrote: BLACK HOLES.

"The existence of black holes was originally discovered by Karl Schwarzschild, a scientist and mathematician. For a black hole to be created, mass has to be compressed enough for it to collapse into itself. There's a mathematical formula which can be applied to the compression and collapse."

Daniel turned and wrote, DNA on the board.

"The structure of DNA correlates to numbers in the Fibonacci sequence, with an extremely similar ratio. Does anyone know what the Fibonacci sequence is?"

Brian raised his hand and Daniel closed his eyes and put his hand over his forehead to the laughter of the class. "Yes, Brian?"

"Is it the order of courses in which Italians eat their dinners?"

The laughter increased and Daniel moved on.

"The Fibonacci sequence is a series of numbers in which each number is the sum of the two preceding numbers. 0,1, 1, 2, 3, 5, 8, 13, 21...and so on. It's present in many other areas in nature, rabbit breeding patterns, snail shells, and even hurricanes."

Daniel returned to the board and wrote, SNOWFLAKES followed by, SPIDER WEBS.

"Both of these are examples of mathematics at work in our world. Each snowflake is unique in terms of its individual structure. However, each arm of a snowflake is identical, causing perfect symmetry. How could they all be unique, yet symmetrical? The answer is that their bonds need to be symmetrical, or they won't be strong enough to stay together. However, each snowflake falls from the sky under unique conditions, causing it to be shaped differently every time. Spiders create webs that are completely symmetrical and almost completely circular. The spider seems to have a natural ability to judge geometrical distance with astounding accuracy. Remember that the next time you kill one for simply appearing in your home."

Daniel placed the chalk down and finished his lecture.

"The universe is an amazing place, made so by its many uses of mathematics. Without these extraordinary numbers, we simply couldn't exist. Everything that happens, every movement, reaction and decision we make, is simply the result of percentages and formulas at work, creating our reality and our ultimate destinations."

The following week came quickly. Daniel sat at the bar waiting for Tim to make his appearance as a familiar, morbid feeling ran through him. He stared into his scotch and felt tears well up in his eyes. He didn't know why those dark fazes overtook him at times. He'd think about his children, his parents, time passing, and the finite reality of life. He thought back to his childhood and having his whole life ahead of him. It seemed like just moments ago, and now he was on the precipice of his fifties. *Maybe Tim was right. Who cares how or why they seem to be reversing the aging process; why not just enjoy it?*

He took another sip of scotch and turned to the television over the bar to distract him from his desolate mood.

"Hey buddy," Tim said as he sauntered up to the bar and claimed the seat next to Daniel.

"Hey, you're late."

"Sorry, I was finishing up an incredible session with Kora. You remember her?"

"You mean one of the three women young enough to be your daughters?"

"Exactly. She's amazing. I swear I get a year younger every time we fuck."

Daniel felt a bit queasy thinking about the whole concept, so quickly changed the subject.

"So, what's our next trip?"

"Well, I've actually narrowed it down to three possibilities."

"Three possibilities? Choose one."

Tim grabbed a napkin from the bar and took a pen from his pocket. He tore it into three sections and scribbled a few words on each one. He then rolled them up and cupped his hands, holding the pieces of graffitied napkin in the center.

"Pick them out. The last one left will be our destination."

Daniel looked at him. "Really? We're going to decide our lot this way—a simple drawing of napkins?"

"Yes, what better way?" Tim said as he held out his hands holding their fate."

Daniel closed his eyes, reached in and grabbed the first material he felt.

Tim hesitated and held Daniel's glance before placing the two remaining napkin balls on the bar and opening the one in his hands.

His eyes grew wide as he read the text.

"Well, this would've been an experience."

"What is it?" Daniel demanded, losing patience.

Tim smiled. "Your first pick, and the first to be eliminated is...deep sea cave diving in Florida."

Daniel looked at Tim. "Seriously?"

"Go on my friend, pick another."

Daniel reached into Tim's hands and grabbed another piece of napkin.

"The second to be eliminated is...whitewater kayaking on the Niagara River Gorge on the New York-Canada line."

Daniel put his hand to his temple. "Are you trying to kill us?"

"Hey, you're the one who wanted to jump out of an airplane."

"That's controlled, with experts. Kayak white water rapids? That's completely unpredictable."

"Everything we do is unpredictable, my man...that's what makes it enjoyable. Unpredictable is intense and invigorating."

"So, what's left?" Daniel said as he nodded his head toward Tim's hand.

Time uncrumpled the last piece of napkin.

"Well, well, my friend. We'll be climbing the famous Mount Washington in New Hampshire with a peak of six-thousand, two-hundred and eighty-eight feet."

Daniel paused a moment to fully take in the uncovered classified information. "Well, it could be worse, I guess. Climbing a mountain doesn't seem like an impossible task."

"Oh, this is no ordinary mountain. It's actually known as the most dangerous smaller sized mountain in the world. One-hundred and thirty casualties have occurred on Mt. Washington since the mid eighteen-hundreds."

"From falling?"

"No, that's what makes this mountain unique. Most are due to hypothermia, and not just in the winter. It sees snow throughout the year. It's not uncommon when severe weather patterns collide and produce notoriously foul weather, which can swiftly move in and totally change the elements. Heavy snow, gale-force winds, sleet and hail can interrupt a seemingly pleasant day in no time. The highest wind velocity ever recorded at any service weather station was registered on Mount Washington."

"Well, are you going to tell me how hard the wind was or just sit there with that stupid look on your face you think I fear?"

Tim glanced around the place as if he were revealing top government information.

"Two hundred and thirty-one miles per hour."

# Chapter Twenty

D aniel sat in the conference room awaiting the announcement of who the panel had chosen to win the Princeton Professor's Grant. His hands were moist with perspiration. He rarely felt this nervous about anything, even the few times he spoke in front of thousands for a dissertation on philosophy. He knew what this meant to Susan and ultimately what her life would be going forward. Daniel didn't teach to make a fortune, although the handsome pay was an added luxury. He didn't teach to help rich, spoiled kids become responsible adults. He didn't teach to give the press a liberal leaning story to write about or to enhance the Princeton public relations. He taught for the Susan Gomes' of the world. Intelligent, gifted, driven, students whose only chance in life is their education. Daniel took a deep breath to calm himself as the chairman of the board, Professor Linda Hodge, entered the room and stood at the small podium at the head of the conference table.

"Good evening board members and thank you for attending. In this envelope is the name of this years' recipient of the P.P.G. grant. I'll now open the envelope and relay the winner's name to you."

The simple movement of Mrs. Hodge's hands ripping open the envelope, holding the paper up to her eyes and communicating the name to the board, seemed to last an eternity to Daniel's awaiting ears. He closed his eyes and listened.

"The winner of this year's P.P.G. grant is...Susan Gomes."

Daniel opened his eyes. It took a few moments before sound returned to his ears. Finally, he was able to hear the clapping and cheers of his colleagues. Professor West turned and offered his hand, which Daniel took and gave an enthusiastic shake. Professor Johnson patted him on the shoulder. A lone tear fell down Daniel's cheek. It wasn't a tear of sadness, fear, or pain. It was an uncontrollable tear of pure emotion, happiness. Not for himself, but for the difference they'd just made in a wonderful young woman's life. Daniel closed his eyes and let it all sink in and felt pure happiness and love. The wave of adrenaline took his breath away and he understood there is no stronger emotion in the world than love.


The first week of April brought the first extended spring weather with temperatures in the upper-fifties. A bright feeling of re-birth settled over the area to fit Daniel's already sparkling mood. There are few feelings on earth as brilliant as the first warm weather of the spring in the north-east, and Daniel basked in the skies' warm glow as he headed home on Friday afternoon. He and Tim would be leaving for New Hampshire and entering the colder weather of the north early the next morning, so he wanted to soak up as much warmth as possible.

Daniel walked into a house filled with poppy dance music as Emily had taken control of the house stereo.

"Hi, Dad," she said, as Daniel kissed the top of her head and sat down next to her.

"Hi, baby girl, how was your day?"

"It was okay."

"How's school?"

"Boring."

Daniel smiled and thought, *that's my daughter, a normal pre-teen girl who already finds school boring.*

"Hey Dad, do you like this music?"

Daniel paused, choosing his words wisely.

"Sure, it's...fun."

"How come you never play it in your car? You always play that old stuff."

"Well, Emily, we are all emotionally linked to the music from our youth. That doesn't mean it's any better than your music, it just means to me it's more enjoyable, just like yours will be when you have children and hear their music."

"Dad, I'm not having kids!"

"Sure you aren't, honey. It's more about how we feel when we're young than the actual music. It reminds us of a simpler time when we're young and free and without worries or responsibilities. It magically transforms us back to feel those same emotions again. We spend the rest of our lives searching for those same feelings to return...to feel young again. Of all the lectures I've given you and all I've tried to teach you, this is of upmost importance and very true— enjoy your youth. It'll be gone before you realize it and you'll miss it forever. Don't be in such a rush to grow up. You'll be an adult for the rest of your life, but once your youth is gone, it's gone forever."

Emily looked at her father as if he sported three heads.

Daniel patted her on the knee.

"Just remember what I said. Twenty years from now you'll say to yourself, Dad was right."

Later that evening, Daniel was preparing for bed, his mind on the trip early the next morning. The pair agreed to drive the seven-hour trek to a hotel at the base of the mountain. Daniel scrubbed his face with cold water and shortly after, collapsed into bed with Madison waiting patiently.

"Hi, handsome, what took you so long?"

Daniel put his arm around his wife, placed a kiss on her lips, and said, "Just sorting out some things in my mind."

"In the bathroom?"

"Well, sure. I do some of my best brainstorming in there," Daniel said, pulling the covers up around his neck.

"Oh no you don't, mister. We're making love before you leave me for the weekend."

Daniel turned over and kissed her and soon they were joined in a passionate embrace. Daniel entered her body and they made love multiple times before they both lay exhausted and satisfied. Madison ran her fingers over his chest through his meager patch of hair.

"So, what was on your mind?"

Daniel held his arm around her body, resting his hand on her hip.

"This trip, where this is all going, and to what end." He glanced down at the top of Madison's head. "For the first time, I'm second guessing my desire to continue."

"Continue the trips with Tim? Why?"

"Come on, Madison, we both know something is going on here that's...abnormal."

"Well, sure, I've noticed the differences in you. Your energy, your youthful glow," she said as she let out a short laugh.

"You think this is funny? I'm seriously confused and, in a way, horrified by it. What if we've stumbled onto something huge here? What if we've created the perfect formula to remain young, not just remain young, but reverse the aging process? What if we've discovered the fountain of youth?"

"I don't know. What if there are things about it that neither of you totally understand yet?"

"Death is a disease, the worst disease, but still just a disease like any other. Why can't there be a cure? What if there is a cure?"

Madison shrugged her shoulders. "If that's reality, then you two will be famous and filthy rich from it."

"I don't want to be filthy rich. I couldn't enjoy my life anymore than I do now with you and the children. Our life is perfect."

Madison hugged him tighter. "I agree. But I, however, think this life is enough. You had doubts, which is why you started these bachelor jaunts to begin with."

"Not anymore. I love you, Mattie."

Moments later they fell sleep in each other's arms, Daniel content and satisfied with their relationship and the life they'd created together.


Tim drove north on I-95 as the sun began its rise in the east and attempted to break through some early morning clouds which brought a few light showers with them. The forecast for New Hampshire called for a mixture of fading sun and clouds and windy with storms possible. As Daniel read the forecast off his phone, Tim just chuckled and said, "Bring it. There's nothing mother nature can produce that can interfere with my climb to the top of that mountain."

Daniel thought Tim's ego had risen to astronomical proportions and wondered if the overabundance of confidence would, at some point, lead to Tim's undoing.

Raindrops fell as they turned onto Hutchinson River Pkwy and entered Connecticut. The sky began to reveal an eerie appearance and Daniel suddenly felt an apprehension in what they were about to attempt. He pushed back into his seat and tried to relax as Tim pushed the accelerator down, picking up speed toward the north and a waiting winter wonderland in the mountains.

They were scaling a steep glacial cirque when suddenly Tim's hold onto the headwall loosened and he fell, sliding down the rock bank. Daniel couldn't tear his eyes from Tim's body as it slammed into a jagged rock, tearing it apart at the waist, his torso falling to the ravine floor while his bottom half stuck on the jagged rock. Daniel turned and vomited down the side of the mountain and when he looked back at what was left of his friend. All he saw was the color red running down the rock wall.

Daniel awoke to the melodic, crisp guitars riffs and soaring vocals of Boston's, *More Than a Feeling*. He turned and glanced over at Tim, who was coolly guiding the car down a long highway.

"Where are we?" Daniel asked.

"Sleeping beauty is awake. We are on I-90 E in Massachusetts. Sill a few hours out."

"I had a fucked-up dream."

"Yeah, about what?"

Daniel looked out the side window and watched as the trees on the side of the highway flew by.

"Let's just say it was pretty grisly and graphic."

"When we pull into North Conway, we can grab some breakfast and settle a bit before hitting Mount Washington."

"Breakfast sounds good. Coffee too. I need some coffee."

"Priscilla will take care of us."

"Priscilla?"

"That's the name of a breakfast diner on White Mountain Highway."

"Do you actually know Priscilla?"

"No."

"Then how do you know she owns it? Maybe it's just a name."

"Seriously, dude? Why would you name a place Priscilla's if that wasn't your name?"

"I have no idea, but is the owner of Wendy's named Wendy? Is Dick's sporting goods owned by a Dick? Is Mike's Hard Lemonade owned by a Mike?"

"I believe the answer is yes to all three."

"You have no clue. You're just guessing."

"Well, why wouldn't they be?"

Daniel just shook his head and decided to drop the subject. The radio DJ introduced *Aqualung* by Jethro Tull, and the melodic, initial guitar riff kicked in and the prodding, harsh, surly voice took over.

"So, is there a Jethro in Jethro Tull?"

"No."

"Okay, then."

"People name bands after other people all the time, but nobody names their business after someone else."

Daniel glanced over.

"You do realize you're insane, right?"

Tim shrugged his shoulders. "Having questionable sanity doesn't mean you're wrong, it means you have an open mind."

Daniel decided to let the argument go and turned up the volume on the radio as *Bohemian Rhapsody* played. He cracked the window to get a bit of fresh air in the car as the sun hid behind cloud cover that seemed to move in all at once.

A few hours passed without much conversation and they both settled into their own thoughts, as the classic rock music played through the speakers. They finally arrived at Priscilla's, pulled into the lot and once inside sat at a small table in front of a large window overlooking the center of the small rural town. A thin, attractive waitress sauntered over and Tim introduced himself and his side-kick before ordering coffee. She quickly returned with two steaming mugs of New Hampshire's best brew.

"What would you fine gentlemen like for breakfast?" she asked with a friendly smile.

"I'll have the Wild Maine Blueberry Pancakes," Tim answered.

"Sure thing, and a very good choice."

Tim beamed as he looked over at Daniel, waiting to hear his friends order, as if their choices were a competition in the breakfast ordering Olympics.

"I'll have the biscuits and gravy with two eggs over-easy, a side of homemade oatmeal, and home fries," Daniel said, his eyes never leaving Tim's.

"Wow, an even better choice. Our biscuits are famous, and you'll just love the oatmeal."

"Why, thank you...Shelby," Daniel said as he read the pretty woman 's name-tag.

She gave him a wink before waltzing away to place their orders. Daniel smiled from ear to ear as Tim just sat with a defeated scowl on his face.

Daniel held up his phone and turned it toward Tim. On the screen were the results of a google search: What to order at Priscilla's in New Hampshire.

"What the fuck, dude. That's cheating."

"I didn't know there were rules."

"Of course there are rules. How can there be a competition without rules?"

Daniel shrugged and smiled, basking in his glorious victory.

Moments later, Shelby returned with two heaping platefuls of food and placed them down in front of their respective owners.

"So, Shelby, who owns this fine establishment?"

"Oh, she's here now if you'd like to talk to her."

"Sure, send her over," Tim said as they both starting to dig into the delicious food.

Shelby walked away and shortly after a heavyset pleasant-looking woman stopped in front of their table.

"HI, I'm Priscilla. Nice to have you today. How's the food?"

"Priscilla, so nice to meet you. The food is superb, thank you. So, you named the place after yourself? How charming."

"Yes, I've always wanted to open my own diner. Finally had the opportunity and jumped at it."

"That's fabulous. We weren't sure whether the owner's name was Priscilla or not. Thank you for clearing that up," Tim said as he beamed and looked at Daniel, who rolled his eyes.

"Why would anyone name a business something that wasn't your name?" Priscilla asked.

"Exactly, Priscilla. Exactly. Thank you for stopping by, dear. You have a wonderful little spot for a diner here and the food is fabulous."

"Thank you, enjoy," Priscilla said as she walked off toward the kitchen.

Tim was glowing.

"Just eat your damn blueberry pancakes, you idiot."

Tim smiled and did just that as he shoved a piece of syrup-soaked pancake into his mouth.

The two ate silently until finished, then ordered a second cup of New Hampshire's best when a local man in farmers jeans, a lived-in flannel shirt and a green John Deere baseball cap approached their table.

"Howdy, guests. You aren't from around here are ya?"

"Hi. No, we're not, actually," Daniel answered.

"Where are ya two from?"

"New Jersey."

"Ahhhh, city folk. What brings you up to these parts?"

"We're going to climb Mount Washington today."

The man nearly fell over and his cap ended up sideways on his oversized head.

"What? You two slickers are going to *attempt* to climb Mount Washington? All by yerselves?"

"Yes, sir."

"Do you find that humorous?" Tim chimed in.

"I'm just concerned for yer safety, is all. City slickers don't usually do well in our parts. Especially ones that have fantasies of conquering the Reaper."

"The Reaper?"

"Ayuh. That's what we locals call her because of her nasty disposition."

"Her?" Tim replied as the farmer just looks at him with his watery pale-blue eyes.

Suddenly, Shelby returned with the coffees.

"Tobias, leave these fine gentlemen alone," she said. Tobias dropped his eyes as if he were scolded and walked back to his counter seat. "Don't mind him, he struggles with accepting outsiders."

"No problem, ma'am. He seems nice enough," Tim said with a smirk which brought laughter from the waitress. "Yeah and I'm the first lady. Enjoy your coffee. I'll be back in a few with your check."

"Thank you," Daniel said. After she walked away, Daniel looked at Tim. "The Reaper?"

Tim waved his hand. "Don't listen to him. He just wants to scare us away. Many of these type of town's local yokels are like that."

"Local yokels?"

"Yup, that's what you call 'em."

Shortly after, Shelby returned with their bill and they were on their way north, headed toward the Reaper and their destiny.


They checked into their hotel, prepared for the climb and were on their way to the Huntington Ravine trail on the east face of Mount Washington. The weather seemed stable for the moment, with cloud cover and moderate temperatures for April in north-east New Hampshire. Tim pulled up to a guide lodge and they entered.

"Howdy," a rugged yet handsome looking man said. Daniel guessed he was someone with unlimited experience in hiking and climbing. He wore a heavy flannel shirt under a bright orange vest. He had a few days growth on his face, but it somehow looked neat and clean, like it always belonged there.

"Hi, I'm Tim and this is Daniel. We're going to hike the Huntington Ravine trail today."

"Hello, my name is Brock. Do you have any experience climbing?"

"Yes, I've climbed a few mountains. We have the gear in my car."

"Okay, you can pick up Tuckerman Ravine Trail just off this road a half a mile up. You can use this lot for parking. Tuckerman will run into Huntington Ravine a few miles up, just follow the yellow markers."

"Sounds good. Any advice?"

Daniel saw a change in Brock's face and for the first time felt like the man was being totally open and honest with them.

"Look, this is a dangerous trail, especially for the inexperienced and the possibility of erratic weather. April can be schizophrenic out there with the different altitudes; bright, calm and sunny one moment, snowy and windy the next. If you come across steep, wet rocks, move around them until you find less elevation that has a solid foothold. Go slow, use your gear religiously, and if you ever feel in danger, please just turn around and come back. You may relax on the way down as many do, having conquered the climb, but the decent is the most dangerous part. Don't let your concentration wane."

"Thank you, Brock, for your concern. We'll remember your advice," Tim said before turning to go.

Brock turned to Daniel. "You have a supply of water and food?"

"We've packed a lunch and some snacks with fluids, yes."

Daniel gave a quick nod to Brock and followed Tim, who was already packing gear into the backpacks.

"We're leaving these here," Tim said, placing the cell phones in the center console.

"What if the car gets stolen?"

"It won't...state of the art alarm," Tim replied, showing his friend the control attached to the fob transmitter. He tucked the transmitter into his backpack and slung it onto his back. He waited for Daniel to do the same. With both packs secured, they headed north up the road towards Tuckerman Ravine Trail. The walk was pleasant as the sun peered out, warming their faces. The temperature hovered around forty degrees and a weak breeze blew from the east. Daniel glanced around at the beautiful landscape. White pine, red oak, hemlock, and aspen-birch trees rules the area as patches of snow appeared as they moved north. A loud, successive *kak, kak, kak,* came from overhead, and Daniel glanced up to see the pale underbelly of a peregrine falcon. The bird hovered for a moment, and then put his slate-blue wings into motion as some sort of prey revealed itself just over the hill.

The duo soon connected onto the Tuckerman Ravine Trail and were hiking over a well-traveled path with a split-rail fence guiding them forward. As they advanced, it seemed they were splitting a beautiful forest of pine trees and the view over the fence was breathtaking. They soon hit rocky terrain and the snow patches gradually became more prominent. Daniel kept his eyes on the rocks on the trail, making sure not to take a wrong step and twist an ankle. The pine trees seemed to be closing in around them as they proceeded as the foliage grew thicker with every step. As they continued, a rustling caught Daniel's attention to the west. He glanced just in time to notice a snowshoe hare scatter over a small stream that had straddled the path. The stream slowly disappeared as they ascended the trail on rocks that appeared to be placed there as steps. Daniel felt a bit of a chill as the temperature seemed to drop by the minute. He pulled his jacket in tight around him and noticed the cloud cover thicken through the trees hanging over them.

"Look ahead," Tim said, turning back to Daniel. A steady stream of rocks heading up a steep incline lay ahead. Tim smiled. "It starts now. You ready for this, old man?"

"We're the same age, moron."

"Yeah but you look, act, and seem older."

"Lead the way, lad."

They climbed the rock passage until it finally levelled off after few hundred feet. They crossed a bridge over shallow river and weaved through a field of boulders, reaching the floor of the ravine. Tim put his hand up and pulled off to the side.

"Let's take a rest, have some water and a snack. Further ahead is the slab."

"What the hell is, 'the slab?'"

"I read up on these trails. The slab is a section of very steep rocks, almost like a rock-wall. Hand and foot placement are very important. However, we have 'the fan' to contend with first."

"The fan, the slab…just what the fuck have you gotten me into?"

Tim laughed, sat on a large boulder and searched his pack for food and drink, pulling out a protein bar and an energy drink. He raised his eyebrows and looked at Daniel.

"I recommend you do the same. You'll need your energy."

Daniel sat beside his friend and followed suit, producing a bag of almonds and a bottle of water.

The sky was completely overcast, and the wind started to kick up in small gusts. The weather was rapidly changing, filling the prophesy of Mount Washington. As Daniel turned to look at what awaited them, he reminisced about everything they had been through and conquered. The Fan, as Tim so affectionately called it, was a large area of broken rock, slowly rising and leading up to the headwall and the slab. The jagged rocks seemed to torment them, from ahead, daring them to attempt the crossing.

Tim noticed Daniel examining the lay of the land, turned to join in his gaze. "It's amazing isn't it? The places this world contains, unseen and un-probed by most. What we've done and accomplished in the last year may well be the highlight of my life. It's made me happier, younger somehow, and I'm eager to continue these quests." Daniel held up his bottle and the pair toasted to their accomplishments as an eager ray of sun fought to break through the thick cloud cover.

They threw their packs onto their backs and started maneuvering over the rocky terrain, being careful with every step. Minutes later, they were safely at the top of a plateau where they turned and took in the view. The ravine spread out in front of them like a picture on a postcard. The pair didn't speak; there was nothing to say as the scene below them spoke in a way that didn't require words. Tim put his hand on Daniel's shoulder and the turned to view the slab, a glacier of grey rock-wall leading to the heavens.

"We're going to climb *that*?" Daniel asked.

"That we are, my friend, that we are," Tim responded.

Daniel examined the one-hundred plus foot granite wall which escalated in what looked like seventy-five or eighty degrees. "Should we don some gear? I mean, this wall is a beast."

"Naaa, let's do this naturally. We should be fine. Just follow my path. The key is to find good hand holds and secure footing. There are three total portions of the slab with ledges in between to rest. The key is to take our time, making sure each contact is secure."

Daniel looked up one last time and nodded. "Okay, let's do this."

Tim nodded back and started his climb, meticulously choosing his path as Daniel watched attentively, then followed, careful to use the same route as Tim. The rock felt cold and hard under his hands, the chill radiating through his climbing gloves. Daniel paused on a secure ridge approximately eight inches wide and watched Tim crawl onto the first ledge and turned to watch his friend catch up. Tim reached his hand down to help Daniel up and they both paused to catch their breath and prepare for the next ascension.

The sun was nowhere to be found as a thick, ominous looking sky peered down at them. The wind surged in manic gusts the higher they climbed and for the first time, Daniel saw a bit of concern on Tim's face, but it vanished quickly as they started the scramble up the next session of granite. Daniel gained confidence with every step, and soon they were one level from the top of the slab. They continued upward, gaining speed as their courage increased. Suddenly, Tim hesitated. He reached a challenging portion of rock-wall which had few hand and foot holds. He extended to the left and slid across the hard granite as he caught hold of the last ledge, pulled himself up and turned to Daniel with a relieved look on his face.

"Daniel be very careful through this part. It's awkward and keeps you off-balance."

Daniel scrambled his way up and reached out for the same hand-hold Tim had used. His back foot slipped as he extended, and he lost his grip momentarily. He felt his heart race, surely a fall from this distance would be lethal. He held tight to his hold and calmed himself before resuming.

"Shit, that was close. You okay?" Tim said from ten feet above.

"Yeah, almost lost it. Just need to make a clean grab to the left." He slid his body over the rock and secured himself on a small-shelf. He then reached up and found the corner of the final ledge above him and pulled with all his might. Tim reached down and grabbed hold of him as Daniel rolled over onto the berm. He rested for a moment before both men stood and looked back over the slab, the granite wall they had conquered together. A fog had rolled in over the valley below and the reflection of the light through the fog onto the land, trees, rivers and trails below was breathtaking. Tim turned and offered his hand to Daniel. They shook in victory as a north-east New Hampshire sky spit out drops of rain.

They continued over a few short scrambles, chimneys, and rock stairs before reaching an avalanche slide which they clambered up. A huge cairn marked the end of the Huntington Ravine Trail and the start of the Alpine Garden Trail, the true summit of their journey. They bumped fists, turned and saluted the slab, the fan and the valley below them. The total hike had taken them just under seven hours.

"Now, we rest, eat and party a bit," Tim said as he kneeled and reached into his backpack, retrieving a bottle scotch and two shot glasses.

"Hey' you didn't tell me this was part of the plan."

"It's a surprise, but after this achievement, we need a bit of celebration. Find a spot to throw a blanket, I'll get out some food."

Daniel unfolded the blanket and found a spot just north of the cairn. A pleasant, open field with a few shrubs and boulders. Tim placed a few paper plates containing cheese and crackers, bananas, and protein bars, along with an assortment of nuts and dried fruit. The pair dug into the food while drinking the bottle of scotch and the light rain changed over to flurries. Tim started to pack up as Daniel took his last sips of golden liquid. He thought this to be their pinnacle achievement, not the hardest or most dangerous, but still the pinnacle, nonetheless. Daniel thought there was a special feeling you got from conquering nature, beating it at its own game and defeating the best it has to offer. It was a rugged, primal, feeling of fulfillment that he'd never forget.

The temperature dropped and the snow intensified, but the consumed liquid in their bellies kept them warm. The mid-afternoon would soon become early evening, so they gathered their things and prepared for the descent and trek back to the guide lodge.

"Going back down the slab will require us to put on some equipment, especially with the wind and snow picking up," Tim said, looking out over the ledge and back down the granite facing. They donned harnesses and readied the rope and rappel devices. They descended slowly, carefully, as the wetness from the new fallen snow made the rock slick and increasingly dangerous to maneuver. After an hour of rappelling, Tim had reached the bottom and waited for Daniel at the very top of the fan. Daniel made his way down but took an errant path that lead to him being about ten feet off the ground without a clear route to the bottom. He suddenly made a decision that would change the day for them both. Instead of re-tracking and finding a safer way to the bottom, he decided to jump the final six feet. As he landed, his ankle slipped on a rock and went sideways. He heard a pop, followed immediately by intense pain.

"Daniel, you all right?" Tim said as he hurried over to assist his friend.

Daniel tried to stand, but his ankle could not bear the weight. He fell back down with his back against the rock wall.

"I can't stand on it."

"Fuck, fuck, fuck! Okay, let me think," Tim said as he looked at Daniel then down the fan running through the route in his mind. "Rest for bit and see if it loosens up for you."

"I think I broke it. I heard a snap and felt something pop."

"Shit, okay. Wait here. I'll make my way back down and get help."

Tim left Daniel with some water and snacks and took out a few blankets from his pack to keep Daniel warm. A gust of wind chilled his face as the snow continued to fall.

"Look at me, I'll be back soon. Stay alert and awake."

Suddenly, Tim was gone and he was alone. He pulled the blankets in tight to conserve warmth. His ankle was already numb and his hands and feet were growing cold. As the time passed, he settled his emotions and relaxed. He opened his eyes and took in the scene. The valley was covered in a blanket of virgin snow and the sky was pure white with falling flakes. The wind picked up in violent gusts, waltzing the snow and wintery dreams through the air. He suddenly felt as he did thirty-five years ago as a child during a winter storm. No worrying about shoveling the driveway, no stressing about driving through the mess to get to work or worrying about the inflated heating bills he would receive at the end of the month. He saw and felt a magical display of nature. He saw a family of white-tailed deer below on the tree line, enjoying a walk through the snow. He pulled out his water and took a few sips to stay hydrated, then devoured a protein bar. He shut his eyes and dreamt of winters from long ago.

# Chapter Twenty-One

He awoke to surrounding blackness, the sun having left the night sky. He was shivering, as the temperature must've dropped twenty degrees. The snow had stopped but the wind continued its relentless assault on the mountain. His hands and feet were numb and he had a two-inch blanket of snow covering him. Time passed and he felt himself fading. His breathing slowed and he became drowsy. He started to forget why he was there, laid out against a rock wall at night amongst the wild animals and nature. His mind was slipping into a confused, foggy state and he started to fall asleep.

Suddenly, he heard voices. He opened his eyes and saw beams of light down below illuminating the fan.

"Daniel! Daniel, you okay?"

He heard Tim's voice pulling him out of his foggy state.

"I'm h-h-here," he slurred.

He witnessed five people carefully approach him as he lost consciousness.

His eyes opened and he took in a room where everything was white: the blankets, the walls, the curtains, the cabinets.

"Hello, Daniel."

He turned and a young woman also veiled in white stood by the bed with a pleasant smile on her face.

"W-what h-happened?"

"Everything is all right. You blacked out at the start of hypothermia, but I'm happy to say you're fine now."

"M-my...ankle?"

"The doctors think you tore ligaments, but there's no break. Here, drink this."

She handed him a steaming cup of chicken broth, which Daniel sipped slowly.

"Where am I? What time is it?"

"You're at Memorial Hospital in North Conway, NH. It's three A.M."

"Where's Tim?"

"He'll be back in the morning to pick you up and take you home. We'll do some tests first but if all goes well, you'll be discharged. Now, get some rest."

The nurse dimmed the lights and was gone. Daniel dreamt of viscous, monster mountains with humungous, sharp teeth chasing him.

Daniel passed the tests. They placed his ankle in a walking boot and gave him crutches to use for a week. He was able to put minimal weight on it as the swelling subsided a bit. Tim arrived early the next morning. He walked in as Daniel chewed on eggs and toast.

"He's alive! How are you feeling?"

"I've been better, but I want to get out of here."

"Working on that, may be another half-hour or so."

"Great."

"How's the ankle?"

"Sore, but with crutches and meds, I'll be fine."

"I called Madison last night and filled her in. She was nervous, but I assured her you'd be fine."

"Where's my phone?"

"Still in my car. Finish your breakfast and hang tight, I'll be back to take you out of here."

Shortly after, they were on the road heading south and Daniel made it his priority to call Madison.

She answered on the first ring, her voice high and tight. "Hello?"

"Mattie, it's me. We're on our way back."

"Daniel, I was so worried. How are you, baby?"

"I'm fine, just a sprained ankle. How are the kids?"

"They miss you. I miss you."

"I know, can't wait to see you all. Be home soon. I love you."

"I love you, too. Daniel, this has to stop. Enough is enough."

"I understand, Madison. I have to go now but I'll be home soon."

They said their goodbyes, he hung up and replayed the last year through his mind. He thought of Madison, Emily, and Logan, his priorities, and the future. He knew what he had to do.


Daniel struggled up the front stairs and opened his front door to his waiting children.

"Dad, are you okay?" Emily said as she threw her arms around him.

"Wow, cool!" Logan said, noticing the walking boot. "How long do you have to have that on?"

"I'm fine, a bit sore and swollen but I'm sure it will heal quickly. I'll be in this thing about a week. I've missed you guys."

Daniel hugged them both a bit longer than usual. Madison walked out of the kitchen and joined the group. Daniel stealthily observed the expression on her face.

"Hi, beautiful," he said while pulling her into the group hug. He was relieved to feel her embrace tighten around his waist.

"I have an announcement to make. I'm done with the trips, getaways, and outings. I'll dedicate all my free time to you, my family, who I love so much. Together, we're going to do all the things we've discussed and I've promised."

Madison's face brightened with an enormous smile and the children cheered and hugged their father. Daniel buried his face in Madison's hair and breathed in her familiar aroma, a scent that made him feel like he was home.

Daniel returned to school the following day and taught his classes. By the end of his lectures he was exhausted from relaying the story of the sprained ankle in the White Mountains of New Hampshire. He sat in his office correcting some exams with his crutches by his side when a soft knock resonated on the door.

"Come in."

The door opened and Susan Gomes slowly cantered over to the chair in front of his desk.

"Susan, glad you came. Have a seat." She did and Daniel asked, "How's your dad?"

"He's stable, comfortable. They'll be trying a new treatment on him stating next week. There's a possibility it'll cure the disease, however, it also could accelerate the cancer if it weakens him."

"Well, I'll pray for the best for him and you." Daniel put the papers away and sat back in his chair. "I'm happy to say you'll be attending Princeton University for free, compliments of the Princeton Professor's Grant."

Susan eyes revealed astonishment and disbelief.

"It's real, Susan. No more worries about paying your tuition. That's not all, either. I've started a fund in the name of your dad. There's already over seven thousand dollars deposited, earmarked for your father's medical bills. This isn't a handout, Susan. This isn't charity. This is a selfish notion on my part because I want to see my best student graduate and do great things. Please accept it all without reservation. This is why I teach; *you* are why I teach. So please, let me be a successful teacher."

Susan didn't immediately react. Daniel tried to gauge her reaction by her emotions, but he couldn't tell what she was thinking or feeling.

"Susan, are you okay?"

Suddenly she rose, ran around his desk, sending his crutches tumbling to the floor and threw her arms around him.

"Thank you so much, Mr. Burton!"

"No, thank you, Susan, for giving me a reason to do these things. Congratulations and make the most of this opportunity, as I know you will. All I ask is one stipulation, one condition."

She finally let go and stood up. "Of course, anything!"

"You keep me posted as you chase down your endeavors. That would make me ecstatic."

She held out her hand which Daniel took and shook.

"Deal. I'll fill you in every step of the way."

She then walked out with a spring in her step, a broad smile on her face, and Daniel hoped a new lease on life. He watched her go and basked in the glow of having helped to make a difference in someone's life.

# Chapter Twenty-Two

A week passed and Daniel abandoned the walking boot and crutches. Mid-April brought mild temperatures and bright, promising sunshine. A feeling of re-birth came over Daniel, partly because of the weather and the health of his ankle returning, but also because of the clarity he now saw in his priorities in life. He'd just finished a lecture and waiting on his phone was a text from Tim.

*How's the ankle? Drinks tonight?*

He knew Tim was going to inquire about May's adventure. He decided it was something that had to be communicated in person.

*Ankle's much better, thank you. Be there at six.*

He stepped into Julienne's ten minutes early and instantly ordered a scotch at the bar. This conversation would take a bit of liquid strength. As he waited for his second scotch, Tim walked in.

"No boot, no crutches, you look great!"

"Thank you. I feel much better."

Tim waved for the bartender. "So, have you thought about May?" The bartender placed his scotch in front of him and he quickly took a sip as Tim ordered a beer.

"Listen, Tim, this has been a great run. I had the most fun I've had in my life and memories that'll last a lifetime, but it's come to an end. I can't do it anymore."

Tim gave his friend a steely gaze before swallowing a swig of beer.

"Come on, man, I know it was a close call, but look at us. We look younger, feel younger and are enjoying our lives more than ninety-nine percent of the people on earth. Do you really want that to end?"

"Tim, I almost died. I have a family. I have responsibilities as a father and husband. I need to do right by them, as much as myself."

"Those responsibilities are growing old and feeble, bored with life, until you shrivel up and die one day?"

"Wrinkles, scars, grey hair, they're all there for a reason. They represent wisdom, experience, and strength of survival. Maybe it's natural that we can't have one without the other. Maybe wisdom and youth *can't* mix. I need to be with my family while there's still time."

"Time is an instrument of mortals, a way to document their existence. Immortals don't require the use of it. The objective of cells is to reproduce or live forever. You have children, I don't. I want to be immortal."

"Tim, I'm sorry. I can't continue."

Tim nodded, patted his friend on his back, dropped a fifty on the bar, and walked out. Daniel would never see Tim Roberts again.

* * *

Weeks passed and Daniel settled into his old routines. He taught his classes, parented his children, and was the best husband he could be. He sent a few texts to Tim that were never returned. Spring turned into early summer, and one day in June he received a postcard in the mail. On the front was the picture of a man during what seemed like an endless freefall. Typed in the bottom right hand corner was: *33 MPH!* Daniel turned it over and read:

*Orlando Towers, Johannesburg, South Africa.*

He felt a rush of adrenaline as he looked at the picture of his friend flying through the air like superman. He placed the postcard in his dresser drawer and hoped it would be the first of many more to come.

# Chapter Twenty-Three

D aniel's last lecture of the year had arrived. He wanted to leave a lasting impression on his students and give them something to brood about over summer vacation. He prepared a lecture on a subject he had recently been educated about himself.

"Today, my genius students, we'll be discussing a dark, morbid subject that is unlike any other subjects or concepts. It's an empty hole, a barren wasteland without theory, conception, or conviction. We know absolutely nothing of this subject, so any discussion relating to it will be purely speculative. However, we are philosophers. Our job is to speculate, to open our minds and welcome thought, whether the thought be rational, abstract, or purely speculative based on emotion, deduction, or simply hope. This subject is death, my friends. Without going any further, tell me what that word means to you, and no need to raise hands...just blurt out your thoughts."

The students all gazed upon him as if he were mentally unstable.

"Come on, no need to be shy now. Speak up."

"Nothingness."

"Fear."

"Uncertainty."

"Peace."

"Heaven."

"Hell," Blurted out Brian, which brought some laughter and levity to the serious, somber mood of the room.

"Silence."

"Mystery."

"Fresh start."

"Freedom."

Daniel put his hand up to quiet the responses.

"What makes this an amazing discussion is the wide range of answers you gave as a group. This is a mature subject and I'd like to explore it further, however, I don't want any arguing, ridiculing, or insulting. If I must shut it down, you all will be reading textbooks for the final thirty minutes of the class. Understood?"

The students all nodded their heads in agreement.

"Good. Now let's continue. You can see how the different thought processes affect the answers. Religion, science, belief in re-incarnation, all play a part." Daniel paused to gather his thoughts. "Thinking about the prospect of one's own death is a constant meditation of our own ignorance. We can't understand death because death can't be known to the living. Birth and death are the bookends of our lives. As soon as we're born, we're dying. However, constantly moving towards death in the framework of time gives life a direction and a framework within which to understand the phases and changes life will bring. The way we experience our world changes as we age. Our senses accept stimuli differently. What we see, feel, hear, taste, and touch change through the years. Time changes. The old look back, the young look forward. What's important to us changes and death is the trigger for these changes. Death isn't real to you, my students...yet, but I assure you, it's becoming very real to me." He paced the room, stopping at the front of his desk and leaning back against it while making eye contact with every one of his students. He let out a deep breath and continued. "By raise of hands, who here believes in an afterlife, supported by religion?"

Half of the class raised their hands.

"Who believes in re-incarnation?"

Five students raised their hands.

"Who believes our souls are a form of energy and continue on somehow?"

Another three raised their hands.

"Who believes we no longer exist and are gone forever like an extinguished flame?"

The final eight students raised their hands.

"As you can see, many different schools of thought exist just in this classroom. All are important, and all should be taken seriously." Daniel stood straight and paced the front of the room.

"Coming to term with one's own death can bring reflection on life. It brings life more meaning. It immerses us in the moment, knowing the moments are numbered. It can make an aging person who has started to ruminate about the end want to live life to his or her fullest and enjoy every moment that is left. Without death, our lives would hold much less significance. Abraham Lincoln said, 'It's not the years in your life that matter, it's the life in your years.' Respect death, understand it, but use it as a guiding force, a tool to live your lives to the fullest."

Daniel paused and stopped by the window, gazing out into the warm, brilliant sunshine.

"Now, what if I told you we could be immortal?" He turned looking for any answers to his rhetorical question. "Anyone?"

Peter from the back of the room answered, "It's science fiction, there's nothing to think of it because it can't happen."

"Humor me, Peter. What if it could?"

"I'd want to live forever then, sure, who wouldn't?"

"Would you though, really? As we've discussed, without death, our lives and our accomplishments would hold much less significance. It's entirely possible we'd end up bored with our existence and longing to die."

"Isn't everyone's natural instinct to stay alive?" Mary asked.

"Sure, but that's an instinct of animals, who don't know any better. Have our brains advanced to the stage that we may understand our own minds, our own desires, and realize we may need a definitive end to really appreciate the journey and its accomplishments?"

As the period drew to a close, he thanked his students for an engaging, successful year, told the seniors he would see them at graduation and welcomed the underclassmen back the following semester. When the classroom was finally empty, only one thought filled his mind. It was a vision of his friend, traveling the world, immersing his mind and body in everything their incredible world had to offer.

# Chapter Twenty-Four

The summer rolled in and Daniel spent the majority of it with his children. Cookouts, trips to the beach and amusement parks, campfires in the backyard with family and friends, trips to the ice cream parlor, and camp-outs in the tent in the yard became the norm.

The incognito postcards continued to arrive, with the frequency accelerating to once a week. One came from Canada, where Tim rode full-suspension mountain bikes designed to float over rocks and tree roots. One was from Washington, where Tim bungee jumped from three-hundred-sixty-five-feet off the High Steel Bridge. In July, Daniel received a postcard with a picture of Tim taking part in the Running of the Bulls in Spain. He even kayaked over a waterfall in Northern Idaho.

As July turned to August, a heat wave hit the eastern United States and didn't relent until the last week of August. Daniel had started readying himself for the new school year and the new students. The last Saturday of August he slowly sauntered through the heat to the mailbox at the end of their long driveway. He pulled out a few bills, a fashion magazine for Madison, and a flyer from a neighborhood grocery store. He felt a glossy, stiff article on the bottom of the pile and drew it out of the stack. It was another postcard, but this one was different. It was a closeup of his friend on a pink beach in front of a sky-blue ocean. When he took a closer look at his friend he almost stumbled to the concrete driveway. Tim looked as he did over twenty years ago when they were at school together. He'd grown his hair out and it looked...thicker, with his natural dark brown color unbroken by silver streaks. He sported a six-pack where a paunch used to be and his arms were chiseled and strong. His smile revealed straight, white teeth. By his side was a young knockout of twenty years, Daniel guessed. She donned a bikini, showing off her golden skin and hourglass shape. Daniel turned the card over and noticed the origin:

*Harbour Island, Bahamas.*

Daniel slipped the card in his pocket and made his way back up the driveway. When he settled back inside the house, he picked up the phone to give John Sullivan a ring.

"Hello?"

"John, it's Daniel."

"Daniel, how've you been? It's been a while, since...new year's evening, correct?"

"Well, that's why I called. How would you like some company one night before I go back to school? We can catch up."

"Absolutely. Just us or with the lady-fare?"

"Just us."

"Well, next Saturday night Jenny has a date with her parents."

"Perfect, I'll be over by six."

"See you then."

Daniel hung up the phone and pulled the postcard back out. He tucked it into his dresser drawer with the others and spent the rest of the day trying to forget how young Tim looked.

\* \* \*

The week dragged by. Daniel spent as much time as possible with his kids, did some research in his preparation for the following school year and took Madison out to dinner at a high-end Italian restaurant on Friday night. Daniel watched as his wife explored the menu for just the right dish.

"Find anything?"

"It all sounds so good. I think I'm going with the Chicken Marsala."

"That does sound great. Maybe we can share?"

Madison gave him her look that told Daniel she knew exactly what he was up to.

"I mean, only if you want too," he said, putting his hands up in gesture of surrender.

"Well, that depends on what it is you had in mind to order, mister."

A warm smile flashed across his face. "Whatever it is you would like to have, my dear."

"So, are you excited to see John?"

"Sure," Daniel said. He rubbed his forehead and shrugged his shoulders. "Look, it's obvious I intend to discuss Tim with him. He knew us both like brothers back then. I just want to obtain his opinion, I trust the way he thinks, and it may help me to share the story with someone else."

"So, in your understanding, a flexible wife isn't enough?"

"That's not what I meant. Getting another man's perspective, especially one we spent so much time with and are relatively the same age, is important."

"I understand. I was just teasing you, my sensitive husband."

Daniel smirked. "Carbonara."

"Excuse me?" she replied with a confused look.

"What I'll order. Carbonara."

"I've never had it."

"You'll love it, as I will your Marsala."

"Of course you will," she responded with a smile.


Daniel arrived a few minutes early. The lifelong friends poured a couple of drinks and sat in the beautifully landscaped backyard. The weather was perfect for an enjoyable sunset, comfortably mild with a hazy orange sun still peeking over the treetops. John owned five acres of wilderness and watching the sun make its daily trek behind the woodlands was as enjoyable as the scene was beautiful.

"So, Daniel, what's up?"

Daniel glanced at his friend.

"Come on, I know you like a brother. You wouldn't have set up a night for us without the ladies unless you had something on your mind."

Daniel took a swig of scotch. "You're correct, I wouldn't have. I need you to have an open mind about something. You're one of the most analytical thinkers I know, and as much as that gives me confidence in coming to you for sound opinion and advice, it causes me to hesitate with anything that may seem...well, hard to accept."

John laughed.

"Well, it's true."

"Okay, okay, you have my word. I won't discredit what you so desperately have to tell me."

"I wouldn't call it desperate, just curious to get your reaction."

"Shoot, my friend."

Daniel squirmed a bit. He took another drink and stared out at the breathtaking scene in front of him. *Here goes,* he thought.

"It's about Tim and me."

"You aren't lovers are you?"

"Would you be serious for a moment?"

"Sorry, go ahead."

"Do you believe there's any chance that immortality could be...*real?*

"No, we all die. Everything dies. It's just a matter of when."

"What if I told you I have reason to believe otherwise."

"I would need to hear the reason and the *proof.*"

"John, you know the excursions we've been taking?"

"Sure, once a month you two exercise the demons of two American males growing old."

"Well, there's some truth to that, sure. However, it has changed."

Daniel sat up to make sure he had John's full attention. He ran his fingers through his hair and continued. "I have reason to believe it has reversed our aging."

John spit out his drink. "Are you serious? Come on, Daniel. I mean I expect this type of thing from Tim, but not you."

"John, I assure you I'm one hundred percent serious. I wouldn't bring this up to you if I didn't believe it myself. Let me explain."

John waved his hand in a mock gesture that said, *Keep the joke going.*

Daniel looked away at the medley of colors visible through the treetops in the early evening sky. He turned back to John. "Look, I don't blame you for your reaction. I'm sure I would have responded in the same manner a year ago, but I assure you, this is no joke."

John's face turned serious and he put up his hand in an apologetic gesture. "Okay, I'm listening. Go on."

"John, I felt younger, I lost weight, my hair thickened, I was loaded with energy, energy I hadn't felt in twenty years."

"Was? Are you telling me you've ceased in joining him and you've reverted back to your middle-aged self?"

"Not completely. Look at me...do I look like I'm in my mid-forties?" Daniel reached his hand to his inside jacket pocket, searching for something of importance.

"Actually, no. You look great."

Daniel held his hands up in a mock gesture. "Well, connect the dots. You're a highly intelligent intellectual."

"Noticing you've lost a bit of weight, maybe using a new skin cream and popped some hair re-growth pills isn't evidence of reversing time, Daniel."

"Tim's blood pressure dropped," Daniel continued, unmollified. "It's now excellent. He looks younger than me. I've started to revert back to my aged self the further I get away from our activities."

"*Your* activities? As if you've created a formula to beat science and nature? That you two have tapped into a fountain of youth? Come on, man. Can't you see how hard it is to believe this?"

"I know it is." Daniel reached into his pocket and hesitated before pulling out the object in hiding. "How about another drink before we go any further?"

"Sure, not certain what you mean by further, but I'll be right back with refills."

Daniel sighed and finally pulled the secret artifact out of his jacket. He studied it before placing it on John's chair, sat back, closed his eyes and patiently waited for his friend to return.

"Here," John said, handing another scotch to Daniel.

"What's this," he asked as he picked up the object. "Ah, she's beautiful. Was back in our college days? He was always a player with the lady fare."

"Turn it over."

John did as he was instructed, and his face turned white. In his hand was the postcard Tim had sent Daniel from the tropical beach a few weeks ago. On the back of the card, on the top right corner, the postmark read August 19, 2019. He dropped his drink and looked at Daniel in disbelief.

# Chapter Twenty-Five

The last free weekend of the summer was spent visiting the Alpine Adventures ziplining course in New Hampshire, just as Daniel had promised his children. Emily and Logan had the time of their lives and Daniel could notice them changing, evolving, growing up by the day. As Logan came down the last run of zipline, a huge smile broke across his face and he jumped into Daniel's arms. "Dad, that was awesome!"

Neither were frightened of the intimidating heights and when they had completed the course, they wanted to do it all over again.

*This is how it happens if you don't stop and take it all in. You wake up one day and your babies are blossoming adults. I'm committing myself to witnessing and experiencing every step of the way.*

Summer faded away and September rolled in with crisp, cool weather. The postcards kept coming. He received one from Maroon Bells, the twin peaks of the Elk Mountains about twelve miles southwest of Aspen, Colorado. It was the most beautiful display of nature Daniel had ever seen. In the fore-front, wisps of tall golden grass shimmered in the breeze as a beautiful lake gave off the reflection of snow-peaked mountains in the distance. Blue-green pine trees scattered the landscape and where the golden land met the base of the mountain. It looked as if each contrast came from another world. Above, an ice-blue sky watched over the scene with a few wispy, white clouds scattered over the display. Daniel could imagine a creator looking down over the picture and feeling pride in conceiving a genesis so gracefully stunning.

Daniel speculated that Tim's excursions became more of a connection with nature as the next postcard came from somewhere more beautiful than the last. He wondered how Tim could afford to visit all of the places he'd been to, but then remembered Tim came from a family with money and he was always successful in his job as a stockbroker.

One came from Seljalandsfoss, Iceland, and showed one of the most famous waterfalls in the world flowing over a granite cliff and splashing down below into a shallow pond surrounded by green grass and shrubbery. In the sky, a golden yellow-orange sun set behind a large fluffy cloud.

One was from Manarola, Italy, where Tim stood holding a large blue fish which Daniel assumed he'd caught. Behind him was a rocky coastline with a village seemingly growing out of the hilly slabs of natural rock formations. The deep blue water splashed against the granite façade and all the small shacks were painted pleasing shades of yellows, oranges, and tans.

For a moment, while looking over all these fabulous places Daniel felt regret for not being there and experiencing all of this with his friend, however the thought of his children and wife quickly extinguished any remorse. He pulled the last postcard of the fishing village closer to his face to get a better look. Tim looked like he was a young man, maybe nineteen or twenty. He wondered when this reversal of age would stop, or if Tim would stop. He worried about his friend, or maybe he just missed him.

"Welcome to Philosophy 110: critical thinking, 2019/2020. What I'll teach you is the theories of the pillars of philosophy throughout history. Socrates, Plato, Pythagoras, Aristotle, Machiavelli, Descartes, Kant, Marx, Nietzche, Russell, Sartre, and everyone in between. However, this class will be much more than a crash course in the history of philosophy. There will be open discussions on aspects of life I feel are important to your understanding of this world and how we, as practicing philosophers ourselves, view, perceive, and use these discussions to improve how you live and think. Every class will be different, and every class welcomes and requires your participation. Open up your minds, my wonderful disciples, and see how far it can take you..."

Another semester had begun, and Daniel was back doing what he loved—teaching. While the end of a season of teaching brought sorrow in the memories of his favorite students moving on in their education and lives, a new year meant new brains to explore and guide into their adulthood, new favorite students to meet and lecture, and the continued joy of helping his students in living their lives, whenever possible.

Daniel sat back in his chair, his first lecture of the year complete and smiled happily...

For he was exactly where he was meant to be.

# Chapter Twenty-Six

### *Four years later*
### *June of 2023, Princeton Graduation*

Daniel watches as Susan Gomes walks up to the podium as valedictorian of the graduating class. She waits as the applause slowly comes to end. She looks out across the crowd and begins

"Good afternoon mothers and fathers, friends and family, teachers, staff, and graduates of the class of 2023. I could just go back and reminisce about he last four years, however, I think it's more important to focus on where we'll be in the *next* four years. Whether it's creating new laws in the senate, designing new houses, baking bread, or teaching future generations, we all must be sure success is associated with what we do. That word, success, may be different for everyone, but know what it means to you, and strive for it every second along the way.

"Ralph Waldo Emerson once said, 'Do not go where the path may lead; go instead where there is no path and leave a trail.' Let's leave a trail that is unique to each of us.

"I hope that what we've learned here at Princeton serves us well. I'm not talking strictly about the learning that goes on in a classroom either. Here are a few 'gems of knowledge' that I've picked up along the way:

"We're all a work in progress, don't expect to get everything right the first time.

"This is only one small step along the road of life, we need much more to make it in the 'real' world. More drive, more thought, more bravery, determination and grit.

"We need to listen to our seasoned elders, our parents, our teachers, people who've already lived through life experiences. They know far more than we do.

"No one is holding us back. We're the only ones who can limit ourselves. Break through those walls and be the best we can be!

"We made it. We made it through the drama, the tests, the projects, the pressures and disappointments along the way, so congratulations, let's be proud of ourselves and most importantly, don't let these four years be the best of our lives."

Susan pauses and in one glance, seems to catch every eye.

"I'd like to thank my fellow students, the staff here at Princeton, my teachers, friends, and my parents, who sacrificed so much for my education. I love you all. There's one person who I'd like to extend a special thanks to. Without this person, I absolutely would not have been up here today, speaking in front of you all. This person helped me at the lowest point in my life, made it possible for me to continue my studies, and is a major part of why my father is alive today to witness this in person. Thank you, M. Burton, the greatest philosophy teacher in the world!"

Applause and cheers echo and rain down all around the crowd. When the ovation dies down, the commencement continues. Daniel witnesses the handing out of the diplomas. He feels a tingle in his heart as Susan accepts hers.

With the ceremonies complete, Daniel congrats the graduating students as they greet the crowd. Julie and Michael walk up to Daniel.

"Hi, Mr. Burton."

"Hi, Julie, Michael. How's everything?"

"We're great. We just found out Julie is pregnant. We're getting married in the fall and we want you to be there."

"That's great news! Congratulations. I'd love to be there."

"We really couldn't be happier Mr. Burton," Julie says.

Daniel hugs her and shakes Michael's hand. "I'm proud of you, Michael."

"Thank you, sir."

The happy couple walk away, and Daniel starts his trek to the parking lot and his waiting car.

"Mr. Burton!" he hears behind him. Daniel turns and sees Susan running after him with a man following her. She jumps into his arms.

"Susan, congratulations!"

"Mr. Burton, I want you to meet someone. This is my dad, George."

Daniel extends his hand to Mr. Gomes. The man is thin, but not the thin which cancer seems to spread onto its victims. He's a healthy thin, with a bright sparkle in his eyes. Daniel guesses the sparkle is the pride he feels in his amazing daughter. George reaches for his hand, and shakes it with a strong, confident grip.

"Mr. Burton, I want to thank you for all you've done for my daughter and myself. You've changed our lives."

"My pleasure. You have a wonderful daughter who'll do great things in this world."

"Mr. Burton, I have something for you," Susan says, and reaches into her bag. She pulls out a hardcover book and hands it to Daniel.

Daniel reads the cover: *Beating Cancer: The Story of My Experience Helping My Father Defeat the C Word.*

"Wow, Susan, that's amazing!"

"I have a publishing contract. One of the big four. This is the first copy and I want you to have it."

"Thank you, Susan, I don't know what to say. I'll cherish this. Good luck with your writing career."

Susan smiles and heads off with her dad.

When Daniel reaches his car, he pulls the book out and opens it. He flips the pages until he reaches to the acknowledgements.

*This book is for Mr. Burton, thank you, my guardian angel...*

Daniel closes the books and tears flow.

# Chapter Twenty-Seven

## *Five years later*

I t is June 11, 2028, and I'm watching my son Logan pitch his final game of the season for Hunterdon Central High. It's been an amazing senior season and he has received multiple offers for scholarships from schools up and down the east coast, Princeton being one of his suitors. Logan pitched to a 7-0 record, with a .98 ERA and 67 strike-outs. I shade my eyes from the sun's rays as he strikes out the side in the first inning. The crowd cheers, but I just sit and take it all in.

These are the memories we take to our graves.

Emily is in her second year at John Hopkins University, where she majors in neuroscience. My life as a father has come full circle and the joy I feel as a result of the accomplishments of my children is indescribable. A fulfilling life isn't determined by how much money you earn, how many people respect you, or how famous you become, it's about the legacy you leave behind, the people whose lives you have affected positively, and the love you have shared along the way.

Logan walks the first batter in the second, however, he is able to induce a double-play off the bat of the following batter and strikes out the fourth to end the second. Still no score.

Madison and I are still very much in love. We've matured over the years and what we have is stronger than ever. My strengths are her weaknesses, and her strengths are my weaknesses. I really can't envision our relationship being any better.

Hunterdon scores two in the bottom of the second to take a 2-0 lead.

I'm still teaching philosophy, though I can begin to see the end approaching. They've offered me a chair on the board of trustees when my teaching days conclude. I would be in charge of the resources and finances used to recruit the possible future students of the University. I've told them I'll accept, under one condition—I'm able to do some recruiting myself. Uncovering talent, noticing something special in young people has always been a passion of mine.

Logan strikes out two in the third before a fly ball to center ends the top of the third.

Julie and Michael are happily married and awaiting their third child. Michael has become a top engineer and he still sees Dr. Phillips, who continues to give me updates on his state of mind and progress. I'm proud of Michael and ecstatic for the couple.

The game remains 2-0 until the bottom of the fourth. Pete Thorpe hits a solo homer, a majestic shot over the center field fence to extend the Hunterdon lead to 3-0.

John, I'm sorry to say, is currently battling prostate cancer. He prognosis is a positive one though, as he still has a battle ahead of him. He found out late in the cancer cycle because he was too proud to get checked, even though he showed symptoms. We visit often for dinner and conversation. At times he acts like he always has, other times he retires to bed early and we spend the evening solely with Jennifer.

The top of the fifth goes quickly with two batters swinging at the first pitch and grounding out. Logan gets the third looking at a wicked heater at the knees. A feeling of pride overtakes me.

Susan, my Susan, has written three bestsellers and is a world-famous author. She has studied all the newest treatments for cancer and written about the processes. She has personally met with John numerous times and I can honestly say she may have saved his life. The cancer institutes have backed John and his recovery because of Susan and her involvement with the fight against the terrible disease. Her dad is still alive and well, I'm happy to say.

I watch as Logan takes the mound for the top of the sixth. My nerves start to take over as I'd love to see him complete his perfect season without a blemish. He rises to the occasion, striking out the side, all swinging. He now has nine strikeouts.

Which brings me to Tim. The postcards dwindled as time flowed on. The last one I received was in the summer of 2020. He was knelt next to a lion with his arm around the beast. That's all the postcard contained, just that picture, with a postmark from Africa on the back. The lion has his tongue out and looks at ease with Tim. Amazingly, he looks the age of fifteen or sixteen, with no stubble and a full head of hair. There's a glow in his eyes that's only present when we're young, the years extinguishing it as we age. I pull this last post card out every now and then just to look at him in disbelief. I called his office that summer but was informed he had moved on months ago. Where he's gone, what has happened, I can only surmise. Did he push the boundaries too far? Has his life ended? Or, is he still living like a free bird, doing what he wants, when he wants, experiencing life to the fullest and reversing time? I'll probably never know. I miss him. I miss my friend and our times together. May you find the happiness you had searched for. May you continue your quest...may you be *immortal.*

We enter the top of the seventh, still up 3-0. The first batter reaches base as the ball bounces off the third baseman's shin on a routine ground ball. Error. Logan walks the next batter and the tying run comes to the plate. The next batter pops up to second followed by a ground out to first. Two away, 3-0, and the tying run still at the plate. Logan throws the first two off the outside corner but comes back with a perfect pitch painting the inside corner. The next is fouled off on the first base side. Two and two count. The home faithful rise out of their seats. Logan rears back and throws a mid-nineties fastball by the batter for his tenth strikeout, the win and a perfect 8-0 record.

His teammates carry him off the field and as he reaches the dugout glances up at me with a bright smile on his face. I know what that final look means.

*Thank you, Dad, I love you.*

# The End

# Other works By David Boiani

# About the Author

David Boiani is an American author living in Coventry, RI. He writes psychological thrillers. He has four books published. His first book, A Thin Line, and its sequel The Redemption. He also has two short story collection, Dark and Darker Musings. His short story 'The Game of Kings' was chosen to be included in the 2019 association of Rhode Island Authors anthology.

**Visit his website at:** www.authordavidboiani.com

# More from Foundations Book Publishing

### *Reborn* **by Jenna Greene**

The marks on Lexil's skin state she is a Reborn - someone who has lived before. As such, she must toil in service to those who have only one chance at life. Sold at auction, she is fearful but accepting of her new life. Everything changes when she must save a young child from a fate worse than death.

With the help of a new ally named Finn, she flees to the Wastelands. There she struggles to survive, while discovering more about herself, the world, and what it truly means to be Reborn.

### *Destination Death: A Horror Anthology*
### *by Chris Liberty*

They say deep in the dark, unexplored woods of the United States exist monsters that creep in the night; some living, others not, yet still able to creep upon the earth, their tentacles of malice strangling whomever they touch. Are these tales of death and evil just mere ramblings of old men whose vulnerable minds twist into fear after they've had one too many drinks? Or are these stories of dread more fact than fantasy?

# Foundations Book Publishing

Copyright 2016 © Foundations Book Publications Licensing
Brandon, Mississippi 39047
All Rights Reserved

10-9-8-7-6-5-4-3-2-1

Immortal
By David Boiani
Copyright 2020 © David Boiani
All Rights Reserved
ISBN: **978-1-64583-023-8**

www.ingramcontent.com/pod-product-compliance
Lightning Source LLC
Chambersburg PA
CBHW060644260626
47161CB00008B/2997